# PRANKENSTEIN
## by Andy Seed

# PRANKENSTEIN

## by Andy Seed

For Heather Garth Primary School, A.S.
For everyone at William Westley Primary, from RM.

First published in 2014 by Fat Fox Books Ltd

Fox's Den
Wickets, Frittenden Road
Staplehurst, Kent TN12 0DH
www.fatfoxbooks.com

ISBN: 978-0992872830

Fat Fox and associated logos are trademarks and/or
registered trademarks of Fat Fox Books Ltd.

Text copyright © Andy Seed 2014

Illustrations copyright © Richard Morgan 2014

The right of Andy Seed to be identified as the author
and Richard Morgan to be identified as the illustrator
of this work has been asserted.

A CIP catalogue record for this book is available
from the British Library.

Printed and bound by CIP Group (UK) Ltd

# Contents

1   A cucumber on the head   1
2   The Bogblocker surprise   8
3   Granny's adventure   18
4   Stairlift to heaven   29
5   The Twince   35
6   Prank explosion   45
7   Trouble at school   54
8   Chinny down   64
9   The theory   79
10   The experiment   89
11   An eventful sleepover   94
12   The terrible truth   98
13   The ultimate prank   108
14   Ouch!   122
15   Windpipe salad   139
16   More please   150
17   Oliver vs Prankenstein   170
18   Hair raising finale   189
19   Venus tells tales   199
20   Searching for cheese   209
21   Star of tomorrow?   226
22   A deadly pill   247

# 1
# A cucumber on the head

Soapy Thompson woke up with a cucumber
on his head. It was large and green and still
attached to the bush. He blinked a few times
and wondered why his bedroom was so bright
and why the ceiling was made of glass. And
the walls.

Soapy sat up and rubbed his eyes. There
was a family of woodlice in his hair and his
left cheek was encrusted with grotty bits of
compost. He was in the greenhouse. Why?
How? He couldn't remember going to sleep
in the greenhouse. It was a rubbish place to
snooze he decided, flicking a slug off his chin.

Then he worked it out.

Sleepwalking.

He hadn't done it for a while, but for most

of his eleven years Soapy had, for some reason, moved around during the night without waking up. It started when he was a baby – it was sleepcrawling then, of course. Usually when he sleepwalked his dad heard him bumping around and put him back to bed, but he'd never actually gone out of the house before. It could be worse. At least he didn't sleeprun or sleepdance.

Soapy crossed the wet grass of the lawn and went back indoors to find his mum scurrying about in the kitchen. He gave her a fright when he opened the door.

"Pugh! What on earth are you doing? And where have you been in your pyjamas? I thought you were still in bed!"

Soapy hated being called Pugh, even though it was his real name. When he started junior school everyone called him Poo. Then when they got bored with that, the annoying kids called him 'Phew' Thompson and wafted their hands when they walked past. He much preferred Soapy, the nickname his granny had given him when he once forgot to rinse his hair after a shampoo.

"I, er, just had a look at the cucumbers in the greenhouse – they're doing well." He didn't want to mention the sleepwalking, Mum would only make a huge fuss, like she did about everything. In fact, if there was a Great Britain Fuss Team, she would be captain. Or manager.

Soapy's mum narrowed her eyes at him. "Are you telling me the truth? You've never showed any interest in gardening before."

"The cucumbers really are amazing Mum, go and look for yourself." He knew he couldn't get away with a lie. Mum was a lawyer and she knew all about cons and trickery.

"If I wasn't dashing off to work, I'd get to the bottom of this – I'm sure you're up to something." He tried to look innocent, knowing that she would disappear to her office any moment. She was always working was Soapy's mum, and always in a hurry.

Why don't adults play more? Thought Soapy. It's much more fun.

Soapy's mum took a slurp of coffee and grabbed her laptop and coat. "Remember, wholemeal toast without jam and some natural yoghurt with two kinds of fruit. And don't use a sharp knife – get Ivette to cut it. And don't be late for school. Bye."

She scurried out of the door.

Jam? Why does she mention jam? Thought Soapy. We don't have any in the house. Or anything else that tastes nice. He stopped and decided the way he was treated was very unfair. He needed to do something about it.

Ivette walked into the kitchen as Soapy searched the food cupboards for something better than wholemeal toast. She was an au pair from Spain, a student who the family employed to do housework. When she first came Soapy thought his dad was calling her an 'old pear' which didn't make a lot of sense as she was quite young and had no stalk.

"Still trying to find a tasty breakfast, Soapy?" she said. "Face it. You've no chance."

"What are you going to have?"

"Some Cracky Pops, which I bought myself, and maybe a piece of chocolate." She took a large bar of Dairy Lush from her bag and waved it in front of Soapy. "I'll sell you some if you like."

"Hey, aren't you supposed to look after me, not taunt me?"

She smiled. "No, I'm supposed to clean the house. And here, that's a full time job."

It was true, the house was very large – part of what magazines would call 'an exclusive development of luxury homes' (or something equally daft). It was on the edge of town, near the countryside on a boring road called 'The Cloisters'. Several rooms contained weird bits of sculpture which Soapy wasn't allowed to touch. His mum said they were 'original abstract artwork' but quite a few of them looked like dead Teletubbies.

Nor was Soapy allowed to touch the expensive coffee machine in the kitchen or the huge Media

NOTE: A 'Teletubby' is a character from a babies' television show who makes silly noises and has a big fat tummy.

Sphere in the living room or the designer chairs in the dining room or the snooker table in the games room.

Soapy thought that the house was boring and that being an only child was boring too. Ivette was alright really and his dad could be good fun, even if he did spend every weekday at the restaurant he owned in town and all weekend at the golf club. Golf, now that *was* really boring.

In the end he ate a banana for breakfast and, after Ivette had gone upstairs and he was ready for school, he had one last poke through the cupboards before he saw something that gave him an idea, a sneaky idea. But it would have to wait until the weekend.

# 2
# The Bogblocker surprise

On Saturday morning Soapy snuck into the upstairs loo with a box of cling film shoved under his jumper. He locked the door without a sound and lifted the toilet seat. Like everything in his house, the loo was sparkly clean. Taking great care, he pulled a long sheet of cling film from the roll and tried to tear it away using the cutter. It slid off the little plastic teeth and crumpled up.

"Stupid stuff," he murmured. "Cling when I say, not now."

After four more goes Soapy found the right angle and pulled away a sheet of transparent plastic. He put down the box and with great care placed the film across the top of the toilet bowl, stretching it tight and then securing it to the edges. Quietly he lowered the heavy wooden seat and stood up to admire his handiwork.

The Bogblocker Surprise. A classic prank.

He closed his eyes and tried to imagine someone innocently coming in to use the loo. Would it work? Maybe at night, or if someone was in a hurry. He looked at it and gave a dirty giggle, which was interrupted by a voice from somewhere nearby.

"Ivette! Are you in your room?"

Mum, coming up the stairs! Soapy's heart leapt in his chest and he hurled himself down onto his knees and pulled up the seat, ripping away the cling film and scrunching it into his pocket before grabbing the box and ramming it into the cupboard under the washbasin.

The footsteps grew louder then stopped outside the toilet door. Soapy froze.

"Ivette, are you in there?"

"Er, no it's me," said Soapy. "I don't know where she is."

"Well, make sure you don't leave any horrible smells or nasty, er, marks. And open the window and use the air freshener."

"Okay, Mum."

Soapy waited for his mother's footsteps to retreat downstairs before he relaxed and picked up the cling film from the cupboard. He sighed and wished he lived in a house where he could actually play pranks.

Soapy adored pranks. He talked about them, read about them and thought about them all the time. His dreams were full of stink bombs, rubber snakes, itching powder, plastic doo-doo and fake vomit. He longed to be a prankster. He dreamt of being someone full of tricks and practical jokes who could fool his friends and deftly prank his parents. He knew lots of pranks but, well, he'd never actually dared to do one.

Soapy once thought about playing a prank on Ivette but changed his mind. What would happen if he spilt something on the white carpet? Or knocked over one of Mum's Chinese vases? She'd probably take him to court and have him locked up. It wasn't worth it.

So Soapy just imagined the pranks he would like to play if he was a little braver – not so humid, as a school report once called him. Or was it timid? He always got those words mixed up.

On Sunday Soapy lay on his beef dreaming of new practical jokes. It was actually his bed he was lying on but Soapy called it a beef because of his crazy mobile. His dad had been on a business trip abroad somewhere and came back with a present. It was supposed to be a smartphone but actually it was a stupidphone, some kind of cheapo version of a proper expensive one.

The phone was okay for calls, as long as the person's number didn't have a nine in it, but the ringtone was stuck on 'clucking

chicken' and, worst of all, the predictive text was out of control. Whenever Soapy tried to key in a word of more than two letters the phone made a random guess and refused to change it. So when Soapy texted 'bed', the phone said 'beef'. It called a friend a fried egg, a mobile a monocle and Dad a Dartboard.

Soapy became so used to this that he started using these words instead of the real ones. So he called Wednesday werewolf, school Scarborough and homework hooligan. Here's what a typical text exchange with a friend looked like:

Soapy: `Done any prangs today?`

Friend: `You mean like a car crash? No I don't drive, Soapy. I'm 11.`

Soapy: `I meat p r a n k s - it's this stumpy monocle.`

Friend: `Oh yeah, forgot. You mean stupid mobile?`

Soapy: `Yeti`

Friend: `Haha. Did a couple of pranks. Put a grape in my sister's`

shoe and some bubblewrap under
the doormat.

Soapy: Did it worm?

Friend: My sister put peanut
butter in my shoe for revenge
so the grape one backfired.

Soapy: Gross peanut butler trick.
Whack about the doodah?

Friend: The doormat was ace! Mum
came back from the shops and it
went off big time. She thought
the cat was ripping up her exercise
ball again.

Soapy: Coolant.

Soapy sat up as an idea came to him. If he
couldn't prank inside then what about outside?
He trundled down the stairs and outside into
the garden only to find his mum tying fabric
around the trunks of the cherry trees.

She glanced up at him.

"Before you ask it's to prevent bruises when
you're playing out here."

"But I never play in the garden in case I

bend one of your sweet peas. I could go to the park instead, though."

"Certainly not! There are all sorts of vile germs there and it's full of people wearing Wayne

Looney shirts. Anyway, the corners of the swing seats are not rounded enough – I've checked them." It was pointless arguing so he decided to do some annoying instead.

"Mum, can I have a cat?"

She put down the string to make sure he could see her scowl.

"No, they're frightful creatures. They scratch the furniture, spew up hairballs and drag dead birds through the house. Imagine the shock if I came home from a hard day in court and sat on a mangled throstle?"

"But Granny's cat didn't do any of those things."

"I wish you would call her Grandma. But, anyway, Grandma's cat had a much nastier habit, you know that."

Soapy pretended he didn't.

"What habit, Mum?"

"You know perfectly well – it... made smells!"

"You mean fish breath?"

"No, I mean those horrid bottom coughs."

---

NOTE: 'Throstle' is an old and slightly nutty name for a thrush (a song bird).

"But that was because she fed it sardines mixed with humous."

"No cats."

"Well, can we have a camel then?"

"Now you're trying to annoy me."

"Mum, would I do that?"

"Yes, but at least you've reminded me that we need to go to your grandma's in a couple of hours – and remember, you're staying there for the night."

It was at Granny's that the trouble began.

# 3
# Granny's adventure

Soapy had forgotten all about going to Granny's. He did remember that it was all something to do with these Italian people who'd been over to visit Dad's restaurant. They had come round to the house a few weeks ago and brought some gifts for the family including wine and an enormous blue-veined Gorgonzola, which Dad had given to Granny.

Cheese was a problem in the Thompson household because Soapy was allergic to it. Cheese made Soapy go strange colours and caused his eyes to bulge. Not a little bit of bulging – right out on stalks.

NOTE: 'Gorgonzola' is a triple ponky Italian blue cheese.

He once asked Dad how they found out that he was allergic to cheese.

"You touched some when you were a toddler. I remember it very well – you turned orange and started quacking."

"What happened then?"

"Your hair stood on end and you began bouncing up and down like a road drill, and you went all starey. I rushed you to the doctor who did some tests and that was that. No Cheddar or Wensleydale ever again for you. In fact, none for any of us – it's far too risky to have it in the house."

Soapy imagined what had happened that day at the doctor's, giving the conversations a silly twist in his head. Soapy did this a lot – he found his imaginary conversations mischievious and often much more amusing than the real ones.

*Dad: So what did the tests tell you, doctor?*

*Doctor: I'm afraid, Mr Thompson, that your son is allergic to cheese.*

*Dad: But he only touched a piece of Gouda –*

*what would happen to him if he ate some cheese?*

*Doctor: Oh, that would be very serious. That must be avoided at all costs.*

*Dad: But what if he ate some by accident?*

*Doctor: Hmmm, well, first his head would elongate considerably, much like a salami. This would be followed by a rapid swelling of the buttocks. Then he would begin to sing opera. Badly. Finally, he would turn shiny and his bum would drop off.*

*Dad: You mean, doctor, my little Pugh would be bumless?*

*Doctor: Exactly. Now you don't want a bottomless boy, Mr T, none of us does, so you must keep cheese out of the house. Got that?*

*Dad: [Nodding rapidly] Yes, yes – we will.*

The sound of Mum calling woke him up and he headed off to the car to go to Granny's. Granny had rung a week before to thank Mum and Dad for the Gorgonzola and to remind everyone that she hadn't seen her choochy little grandson Soapy for ages (even though it was only three weeks), and if they were coming over anyway why didn't he stay the night?

Granny lived about 20 miles away in another town and they visited her about once a month. She lived on her own in a small house ever since Grandpa had gone out to buy a garden gnome one day seven years ago and never came back.

Soapy liked her but she was annoyingly old and her grey hair only seemed to grow on one side of her head. She always looked as if she'd been standing in a gale for ages. Her house smelt a bit funny as well, and there was rather too much lace around for his taste.

Granny also liked Soapy, and her favourite activity when they were together was to say that when he was a baby he looked like Winston Churchill. She did this about once every fifteen minutes, which kind of wore Soapy down after a while. But she made the best apple pie known to boy and so he forgave her.

Granny was also infirm. Soapy wasn't sure

NOTE: 'Winston Churchill' was Britain's Prime Minister during most of World War II – and looked a bit like a baby.

what infirm was and he sometimes asked
himself why she couldn't be firmer, but he
did know one thing. Being infirm meant that
Granny had an electric stairlift to carry her up
the stairs, and Soapy was occasionally allowed
to go on it if he was good. So even though he
was sorely tempted to try some pranks while
he was away from home, he knew that he
would be banned from the stairlift so it wasn't
worth the risk.

So, after his mother made her usual threats
about behaving politely with Granny and
speaking up and not leaving unwanted things
in the lavatory and eating all his greens
(and any other colours provided) she gave
him a curt kiss and returned home, leaving
Soapy to survive one night alone.

After sprout soup followed by apple pie
heaven, Soapy and Granny watched a wildlife
film about voles and then she fell asleep in
her chair. Soapy watched some snooker then
prodded her with various objects to see what
would wake her. A banana didn't work. Nor

did a slipper.
A rolled
up Daily
Express
made her
snort, and
a finger
made
her open
her mouth
like a fish then
say something about pickled

eggs. But it was her own walking stick
that did it. She awoke with a strange 'foooo'
sound then turned to Soapy.

"Eh? Wha? Right, I think it's time you were
in bed, young man."

"Granny, it's only quarter to eight."

"Do you know that when you were a baby,
Pugh, you looked just like Winston Churchill?"

"I'll go up and brush my teeth. Good night."
Even bed was better than that.

Soapy woke up the next morning with a

volcano of a headache. He wearily lifted his head from the pillow and felt a lumpy thud inside his brain like there was a rhino in there trying to get out.

Oooouugghh.

He strained open a crusty eye and saw bright light behind the curtains. It was morning, but what time? He lifted himself out of the bed slowly, his whole body creaking. I've never felt like this before – I wonder if I'm ill? He sidled to the door and opened it. There was a strange smell on the landing.

"Granny?"

Silence.

"Granny, you there? It's Soapy."

There was no answer so Soapy stumbled across the landing and tapped on her bedroom door. Again, there was no reply so he turned the handle and went in. The curtains were open and the bed was made. There was lots of lace but no sign of Granny.

Unsteadily, Soapy made his way downstairs, his crusty eyes still half-closed, and into the

kitchen. She wasn't there. She wasn't in the
living room, either. There was only the strange
smell but it wasn't the usual one – this was
more like burning.

"Granny!"

Maybe she'd gone outside to feed the birds or
something. The back garden was quite long –
she could be down at the bottom or in the shed.
He decided to get dressed and have a look.

Then he noticed it.

Just at the moment that he trod on the first
step of the stairs.

The stairlift was gone.

He opened his eyes fully but it wasn't at the
bottom of the staircase and it wasn't at the
top either. And there were weird sort of burn
marks all along the metal rail on which it moved.

Soapy ignored his aching joints and scampered
up the stairs. There was a large ragged hole in
the ceiling of the landing. He was sure that it
wasn't there yesterday. He couldn't make out
anything in the darkness of the hole.

"Granny!"

And then he just caught a tiny low moan coming from above.

"Granny? Is that you?"

There was more moaning – it was definitely her. Soapy ran to find his mobile and called 999.

# 4
# Stairlift to heaven

Soapy's mum and dad arrived just as
Granny was being carried out of her house on
a stretcher. There were lots of questions and
flapping but the ambulance driver managed
to calm Soapy's mum down.

"It's alright Mrs Thompson, there are no
serious injuries. She just has bruised ankles,
a sprained chin and a twisted lip. Oh, and
one of her toes got stuck up a nostril too, but
we got it out. She'll be fine."

Soapy's mum didn't
look convinced but Dad
made a cup of tea and
told Soapy to sit down
in the kitchen to tell him
what had happened.

Soapy tried to think where to start – at least his headache had now gone. Dad peered into the hallway. There were lots of hefty police officers bumping around upstairs.

"So, you woke up and you couldn't find Granny, is that right?"

"I checked every room and she wasn't anywhere then I noticed the massive hole in the ceiling at the top of the stairs and I heard a noise that sounded like her."

"You did the right thing to call an ambulance right away – well done." It made a pleasant change to get some praise from a parent, thought Soapy. He was just about to explain that the stairlift was missing when a policewoman stuck her head into the kitchen.

"Do I detect tea?" she said, twitching her nose. "I was wondering when the kettle would go on." Dad took the hint.

"Oh yes, of course, er, officer. Would you all like tea? Or maybe coffee? How many of you are there up there?"

"Oh, how kind. Well there's Sergeant Pinnock

who likes black coffee; there's Constable Moafy – he likes strong tea; then there's Constable Dodds who prefers Bovril, and there's me – I'll go for something herbal or a soft fruit blend."

While Dad started shuffling about in the cupboards Soapy asked the policewoman what had injured Granny.

"Well, we're still conducting our enquiries, of course, but we think that there may have been an electrical fault with your grandmother's stairlift – possibly a power surge."

"You mean she was sitting on it when it shot through the ceiling?"

"Well, it does look that way, yes."

Dad emerged from a cupboard covered in dust and cobwebs. He was holding an ancient tin.

"Can't find any coffee but there's this Fludge's Dandelion and Acorn Extract. Oh. Best before 1946."

Before anyone could answer there was a loud thump from upstairs and the shout of voices telling each other to lift slowly. After more bangs and bumps a beefy policeman appeared, wiping his brow and looking round.

"Mr Thompson – could I have a word please?"
He disappeared into the living room followed by
Dad and the policewoman. They shut the door
but Soapy couldn't resist putting his ear against
it. The voices were muffled but just audible.

"...the lift went out of control..."

"...it's a wonder she wasn't mashed..."

"...travelling at high speed..."

"...took off like a missile..."

Then Soapy noticed the keyhole. He put his
ear to it and the voices became much clearer.
His mum was in there too and was asking
questions with the burly policeman doing his
best to answer.

"But surely stairlifts don't normally launch
elderly ladies through the roofs of houses, do they?"

"I've only come across it a few times, true.
It's most odd indeed. But I haven't yet told you
the strangest thing we found."

"What do you mean, officer?"

"Well, I'm not really sure how to put this,
but the stairlift had been, er, modified."

"Modified? What do you mean – changed?"

"I mean more than changed, Mrs Thompson. It was souped up."

Dad joined in the questions.

"Souped up? In what way?"

"I mean that someone had fitted a V8 engine, twin exhausts and a Recaro seat, sir. It even had a sat nav."

There was a moment of silence then Mum blurted out, "I want to see this for myself!" Soapy heard the sound of everyone standing and moving for the door. He hurled himself into the kitchen and looked down, trying to act normal as the four adults bustled up the stairs.

Soaped desperately wanted to follow them – he just had to see the souped-up stairlift, but something stopped him. Whilst he was looking down, he noticed a speck on the kitchen floor, then another. There were several small pieces of something crumbly and white.

Soapy bent down for a closer look. There were distinctive blue veins amid the white crumbs.

It was Gorgonzola cheese.

# 5
# The Twince

Granny was recovering in hospital and Soapy was back at home. Dad had gone to the golf course, as usual on a Sunday, and Mum was rushing about. She was in a mood because Soapy had invited two friends around to play and that meant that she had to keep an eye on them when she wanted to get on with some work. Soapy was keen to play Scalextric.

"We'll be really quiet Mum, honest."

"Those cars fly all over the place – I don't think my nerves could stand it if anyone received a bruise, especially after this morning's fiasco. I'll find you something nice and quiet to do."

Soapy was just about to protest when the doorbell rang. It was Arvo and Loogi, 'the Twince', as Soapy called them. Arvo and Loogi were twin brothers from Estonia, near Russia. They had moved to the UK two years ago, and had become Soapy's best friends. They were tall and polite and looked almost identical. One of the things that Soapy liked about them was that they had unusual interests. Arvo always carried round a small collection of bones. His pockets bulged with bits of mouse skeleton, rabbit ribs and bird skulls. Loogi, meanwhile, was quieter and cleverer than his brother and usually had a crossword in his hand. He often bumped into things as he wandered round with his head down trying to solve clues, while Arvo was famous at school for his catchphrase, 'I can feel it in my bonce' Although their English was good in many ways, they did have a strong accent and a curious way of speaking which often amused Soapy.

Half an hour later the boys were sitting in the kitchen, drawing a vase of flowers. This had kindly been set up by Soapy's mum as a less dangerous alternative to Scalextric. Soapy and Arvo were deeply bored but Loogi was enjoying it – he liked drawing. Mrs Thompson arrived to check that no violence had been done with the lilies.

"That's good, Loogi. Yours is, erm, interesting too, Arvo. What have you drawn, Pugh, one of the battles of the Boer War?" He didn't answer.

---

NOTE: 'Bonce' is the way the Twince pronounce bones in their Estonian accent.

Loogi looked up. "Mrs Thompson, do you have a pencil sharpener? My pencil is now blunt".

"Pencil sharpener? Certainly not – those have vicious blades. I blunted the pencils deliberately, anyway."

"But I do better drawing with a sharp pencil."

"Pencils are dangerous, Loogi. They could have someone's eye out."

Soapy groaned inside. His mum was always like this when his friends came round. He put his fingers in his ears and continued an imaginary version of the conversation.

*Loogi: But I will be very careful.*

*Mum: That's all very well, Loogi but only last week I was in court dealing with a case where someone's eye was out.*

*Loogi: What happened?*

*Mum: It was a nasty incident involving unauthorised gouging and aggravated poking. Not only was the eye out but it took nine hours to decide who should put it back in. So no pencil sharpeners. And don't knock over the vase, although it is a rubber one just in case.*

"Soapy!" It was Arvo. "Your mum has gone."

He took his fingers out of his ears. "Sorry about that. Mum can't help it sometimes – she's a barrister."

"What is a barrister?"

"It's a kind of lawyer – she works in a court."

"A lawyer? You mean like Lionel Hutz on the Simpsons? Cooool."

"Arvo, my mother is nothing like Lionel Hutz. He's funny and silly. My mum is sensible and safe. She is dangerously safe."

Loogi looked up. "But how can a person make danger and safety?"

"I was playing with words, don't worry about it," said Soapy.

"OK, if you teach me this game sometime – I want to play word too."

"Er, right..."

Arvo folded his sketch in half. "Now that your mother is gone do we have to be drawing still?"

Soapy slapped his pencil onto the paper.

"No. I've had enough of flowers. Come on you two – let's go up to my room – I need to tell you about something really odd."

The brothers listened with wide eyes as Soapy explained in great detail what had happened at Granny's. He described the huge hole in the ceiling and the ambulance's arrival and the police's peculiar discovery upstairs.

He then went through the conversation he'd overheard in Granny's living room and he even told them about the Gorgonzola cheese, something he hadn't mentioned to his parents or the police.

"I checked in the fridge and the whole thing was gone. The only trace of it was the crumbs on the kitchen floor."

Arvo creased his brow. "What I am not understanding is how the stairlift change could have been. It was normal when you arrived, you say?"

"That's right it was. I even went up the stairs on it when I went to bed."

"So, the modifyings must have been happening in the night, but how?"

Loogi looked at them both and said what they were all thinking. "And who?"

The Twince agreed that it was a mystery and that it should be investigated right away. They decided that the police needed help and that they were the best people to do it.

"I am expert in following clues and solving puzzles," announced Loogi.

"This isn't a crossword," said Soapy. "My granny was nearly rocketed through her roof by some maniac with motor repair skills and a liking for late-night toasties."

Arvo nodded. "It is indeed strange but we are your friends so we can keep an eyeball on you and watch out for this nut of the dangerous sort."

"And perhaps we can visit the house of your granny and seek evidences?" said Loogi.

Soapy looked at them and took a deep
breath. "Maybe. But there's one more thing
I haven't told anyone. I discovered it when
we arrived back home at lunchtime."

The brothers leaned forward. "What?"

"Well, I took a small overnight bag to Granny's
with my pyjamas and a change of clothes and
my toothbrush and stuff. As soon as we got
home today, Mum told me to go and unpack
it." Soapy turned around and checked that
the door was closed.

Arvo's voice was low and dark. "Ah, was
something missing there?"

"No, there was nothing missing. Something
had been added."

"You mean a person put in your bag a thing?"
said Loogi.

"Yes. It was something else very strange.
A bag of Mini-Bel Cheeses."

"Are you meaning those little round ones
that have the cover of wax?" said Arvo.

"That's right. They're Granny's favourite."

Loogi crumpled his lip in puzzlement.

"You have the cheese allergy, I know. What did you do with them?"

"I was going to throw them in the bin but Mum might have found them. She would have gone spare finding cheese in the house – and she would never have believed that someone hid them in my bag. So I sneaked them outside and hid them in a plant pot in the shed."

"Thinking good," said Arvo.

Loogi scratched an ear. "Could your granny have put them in the bag?"

Soapy shook his head. "Definitely not – she knows I'm allergic to cheese and is always careful to keep it away from me."

Arvo stood up and put his hands in his pockets. "We will help you solve this mystery, Soapy. I can feel it in my bonce!"

# 6

# Prank explosion

Soapy hated Monday mornings. He didn't mind going to Scarborough, as he and his mobile called school, or even getting up early – it was all his parents' rushing and fussing that was the problem. They both had to get ready for work and they were never in a good mood.

On this Monday, it started at ten past seven, when Soapy's mum stomped into the kitchen in her bathrobe, grabbing the kettle and muttering about her alarm clock battery going flat.

"It has those silly little batteries that nobody ever has in the house. Now I'm late and there's an important meeting with Sir Philip at 8.45. And where's Ivette? – she should have made some coffee."

Soapy looked at his mum as she turned round. There was something on the back of her bathrobe – a dark patch of a nasty looking substance.

"Mum, what's that on the back of your dressing gown?"

"What? I'm really in a hurry, Pugh. Please don't talk to me unless it's important."

Soapy was considering whether it was important or not when his mum perched herself on a tall wooden stool and scribbled something on a note pad. She wouldn't listen even if he did tell her.

Soapy opened the cereal cupboard dreaming that there might be some Frostiloops or Choco-Krisps in there, knowing he would only find Wild Porridge and Total Bran. He decided to go for toast. Just as he opened the bread there was a deep wail from upstairs.

"Eurrrghhhhh!"

It was Dad. Seconds later there were hurried footsteps on the landing and a booming shout. "Soapy! Did you put ink in my shower gel?"

He was going to say 'no' when Dad yelled again.

"Ivette? Can I borrow some make-up remover? My face is bright green!"

Soapy was just about to go upstairs for a look when Dad came pounding down in his dressing gown and bumped into him. His face was the colour of a lettuce.

"It wasn't me, dart- I mean Dad, honestly.'

"Well who did it then? And where is Ivette and your mother?"

Soapy's mum spoke before he could answer.

"Jake, why is your face painted green? – you look like one of those silly men who stand still and scare children in the shopping centre."

There was a scraping noise and Dad stared at his wife as she stood up. "And why are you dragging a stool about?"

She frowned, turned around and saw that her bathrobe was glued to the stool and wouldn't come off. "What is going on?" She pulled at the stool and heard the expensive towelling fabric tear.

"Whoever did this is going to be the sorriest person in the world!" She grunted and tugged at the seat again causing it to bash against the cooker. It wouldn't shift.

Dad turned to Soapy. "What is going on, young man? Tell me now."

He gulped. "Nothing... I don't know, really. I just know it wasn't me – I haven't done anything. I wouldn't dare."

The last words seemed to have a calming effect on his father. "Hmm, well, who could it have been then? I'm sure that Ivette wouldn't risk getting fired by playing stupid pranks like this. Where is she, anyway?"

She appeared right then. Her face was sweaty and she was holding up what looked like a great long washing line made up of bras, pants, and satin thong things that Soapy had never seen before. She puffed out her cheeks.

"Someone has sewn all my underwear together!"

Soapy gave out a tiny splutter then bit his lip. Dad stifled a grin.

Ivette snorted with tight lips.

"I am supposed to be seeing Marco this lunchtime. What am I going to do? I am not going to meet my boyfriend in a pub with unwashed knickers!"

Nobody knew what to say. Ivette looked at Soapy for signs of guilt, then at Dad.

"Mr Thompson, are you very sick?"

"I'm sick of all this messing around," he said. "We'll get to the bottom of it but I've got to get to work. Ivette, have you some face scrub or something that'll stop me looking like an alien?"

"Er, yes, probably but Mrs Thompson did you kno..."

"...That a stool is stuck to my bottom? Yes." And she stomped out of the room with the tall

---

NOTE: 'Satin thong things' are very tiny knickers that make Soapy (and his dad) blush.

chair bashing against the door frame
as she went.

Soapy had seen enough. He made the excuse
that he had to get ready for school and then
skipped upstairs and into his room. He closed
the door and looked for his mobile to text Arvo
and Loogi about the morning's crazy events.
His mind was buzzing. What was going on?
Who was doing this and why? Was he next?
There's textbook pranking going on – in my
own house! Soapy didn't know whether to
enjoy it or not.

The phone was nowhere to be found. Soapy
checked the windowsill and heard a commotion
outside. A man with a dog was passing the
house. He stopped to stare at his dad's Jaguar
which was parked in the drive. It was almost
entirely enveloped by birds, about thirty
pigeons, plus blackbirds, thrushes, sparrows
and even a gull. The dog yapped and all of
them took off in a crashing flurry of wings
and squawks.

The car was covered in bird seed.

And with all those birds, that wasn't the only thing it was covered in.

Soapy dropped onto his bed. He had to find his mobile. He looked under the bed, on top of the wardrobe and in his drawers. Nothing. Maybe it had fallen in the bin? He picked it up and shuffled through the contents. There was no mobile phone but he did find some other things. A tube of superglue, a needle and thread, and an empty packet of bird seed.

What is going on?

Soapy's heart was pounding as he hid the evidence in his schoolbag. He sneaked downstairs and rang his mobile from the house phone. It was in his pocket.

# 7
# Trouble at school

School began, as it always did, with assembly. While they were queuing up to go into the hall, Arvo and Loogi asked Soapy to explain his latest text which they hadn't really understood.

`Someone glued a stooge to Mum's bottleopener and dyed Dad's fake greeny. Ivette's knick-nacks are all sewage together.`

The Twince' eyes were wide as Soapy translated. He expected them to laugh but instead they gave each other a pondering look.

"So the pranks are continuing at your house?" said Loogi. "That is most interesting."

Soapy told them about the things he found in his bin.

"Whoever did it wants to blame me, I reckon.

What about you two — have there been any mystery pranks at your house?"

Arvo sighed. "I wish there were. Instead we are having to see our parents dressing in the clothes of the stupid. Mother she wore a mini-skirt and father put on this thing called a gold disco suit."

"They were attending something called a Six Tonight, I think?" said Loogi.

"A what?" said Soapy.

"It is a crazy dance thing with the hippy and big flares," said Arvo.

Soapy smiled and hooted. "Oh, you mean a Sixties night."

"Yes, Sixties Tonight, but they thought it would be smart to dress like that all day." He made a puking face just as Mr Eckersleight, the Headteacher, walked past.

"Please don't do that, Loopy. We're going into the hall now."

Mr Eckersleight always called him Loopy, but he was well-meaning so the Twince never complained too much.

The assembly was about heroes. Mr Eckersleight told the story of a woman who had raised £18,000 for the blind by sitting in a bowl of chicken soup for a week. Soapy half-listened, studying Mr Eckersleight's hair as he spoke. Everyone in the class said that he wore a wig and it did seem strange that his hair was black and straight on top but grey and curly at the sides and the back. But anyway, no one at the school made fun of Mr E because he was kind.

Unlike Mr Chinn.

Mr Chinn was Soapy's teacher. His mobile called him Mr Chipboard but all the other kids in the class called him 'Chinny'. It was a useless name because Mr Chinn actually had no chin at all, just a sort of flap between his lower lip and his neck. Later, during maths, Soapy was thinking that maybe they should call him 'Flappy' when he realised that everyone in the classroom was looking at him.

"Well?" said Chinny.

"Er, sorry, I missed the question"

"I suppose I'd better repeat it then. What is 52 divided by 4?"

Soapy's brain refused to engage. He was quite good at maths but Mr Chinn just made him nervy. "Erm... 17?"

"Wrong. Try again."

"It's, er, it's 19."

Several other kids had their hands up but Chinny ignored them. "It is not 19. Oh, come on, Thompson, even some of the infants can work it out."

Arvo wrote 13 on a page of his jotter and managed to flash it in Soapy's direction without Chinny noticing. It was right.

Now try to stop daydreaming, he told himself.

Lunchtime wasn't any better; in fact it was worse. Soapy had to sit on the Allergy Table in the hall with three little kids. Not only that but he also had to wear a big label hanging from his neck with 'NO CHEESE' written on it. Mind you, that was better than the girl opposite who had 'NO NUTS'.

It was bad enough that Soapy couldn't sit with his friends during dinner but he also had to endure everyone walking past and making fun of him. Well, it wasn't quite everyone, it was mainly one person – a girl in his class called Venus Bray.

Venus liked to save bits of mashed potato on her plate and flick them at Soapy when she walked past. She also called him Cheeseboy and laughed at his mobile with her friends. Annoyingly, she was very popular as well as being big, loud, rude and mean. It was no good telling Chinny about her constant taunts – Chinny believed that every child had to stand up for himself. And

Soapy's mum and dad were friends with Venus's parents which didn't help at all.

He did once complain to Mr Eckersleight about her but he just went on about what a wonderful singer she was in all the school's drama performances and in the choir.

"And did you know that Venus has already made it through two rounds of Stars of Tomorrow on the BBC? That means she might be on television – isn't that wonderful?"

It wasn't wonderful and he did know because everyone went on about it, not least Venus. Like just then.

"Oi, Cheeseboy, did you know I'm gonna be on telly?" She pretended to flick a bogie at

him. He turned away – there was no point in responding.

At least in the afternoon it was PE. Soapy liked PE except when Chinny made them go outside in cold weather wearing just shorts and a t-shirt. Like today.

"Come on, get changed quickly!" He produced a stopwatch from his pocket. "I'm giving you exactly two minutes or it's extra homework."

Soapy scrabbled about in his PE bag for his kit and pulled out the required items, a little manky, but all there. As he undressed there was a commotion behind him. Lots of kids were laughing at Arvo and Loogi. Soapy climbed on to the coat stand to see.

"I didn't place this in my bag. Was it you, Loogi?" Arvo was holding up some shiny piece of clothing.

"Of not course, and I did not exchange my shorts for this miniature skirt either." He held up a pink mini-skirt and everyone cackled, including Soapy.

"Stop that racket!" Chinny pushed through and snatched the mini-skirt and disco suit from the Twince. He fixed the boys with a glare. "Did you bring these?"

"No, they were in our PE bags." said Arvo. "Our shorts are missing."

"Oh are they just? Well, it looks like you

jokers will have to wear these instead."

"But these belong to our parents." said Loogi. "They are larger than we require."

"And they are giving of the embarrassment, much," added Arvo nervously.

"I'm not here to argue," blasted Chinny. "Just put them on."

Every member of the class stood still in silence, waiting to see what would happen.

Soapy couldn't bear it. "I think there was a mix-up at home, Mr Chinn. Maybe they could wear some shorts from lost property instead."

"How dare you tell me how to organise my lessons and impose discipline!" Chinny's nostrils were flaring like a gorilla's.

Big mistake.

The teacher smiled unexpectedly. "I'll tell you what, Thompson. You can wear this instead." He threw the mini-skirt at Soapy. "You've now got eleven seconds to get changed or it's double homework."

# 8
# Chinny down

Playing football at school in a mini-skirt wasn't something Soapy wanted to do again. Or even remember. Ever.

He slept a troubled sleep that night and woke up once more with a slight headache. Today has to be better than yesterday.

It was and it wasn't. It was because the mysterious pranks kept happening, which made Soapy laugh with glee, and it wasn't because he was worried that he would be the next victim.

It began at school when Chinny walked into the classroom, unusually late. He looked very peculiar indeed and there was a lot of sly nudging in the class, although nobody dared to say anything. Finally he spoke.

"Shorry I'm late thish morning, clash. Letsh do the regishter quickly."

Soapy looked at Arvo. Why's he talking like Sean Connery?

And there was something not right about his mouth or, to be more exact, his teeth. They were somehow bigger than before. Much bigger. He looked like a cartoon horse. Chinny was just about to sit at his desk when he noticed that everyone was staring at him.

"I can shee that you've all notished that I'm shpeaking in a rather shtrange way. I'm afraid it'sh becaush I shomehow put the wrong denturesh in thish morning. I don't know how it could have happened but theshe onesh are not mine."

Venus put up her hand. "What are denturesh, Mr Chinn?"

"They're not called denturesh, they're denturesh."

"But I said denturesh."

Chinny scowled. "Oh, never mind, they're falsh teeth."

Soapy tried not to stare but he couldn't help it. The rest of the class were just the same. Everyone was putting in a gigantic effort not to laugh.

Chinny sat down and pulled open the drawer of his desk to take out the register. Except he pulled off the knob instead. The drawer was stuck.

"Who hash done thish?" His face took on the colour of blood. "Shomeone ish playing tricksh on me!" All thirty two children looked down in a flash.

The morning continued in the same way. When Chinny told someone to give out the history textbooks on the shelf, they weren't history textbooks at all – they were all Beano annuals. He was trembling, with a rising chest, when the school secretary, Mrs Wope, knocked on the door and walked over to his desk.

"Did you order some paper clips, Mr Chinn?"

"Yesh, have they arrived?"

"Well they have but there's rather a lot of them. Is there, er, something wrong with your teeth?"

Chinny turned away and covered his mouth with a hand. "Pleashe jusht bring the paperclipsh in Mrsh Wope."

She left the room then came back two minutes later with ten large boxes of paper clips. Then she brought some more. And some more. Half an hour later there were 850 boxes of Jumbo Clips blocking out light from the windows. Chinny held his head in his hands and let the class go out to play five minutes early.

Soapy grabbed Arvo and Loogi and headed into a quiet corner of the playground.

"Will someone tell me what is going on with all these pranks. Who is doing them?"

The brothers held out their hands. Then Loogi furrowed his brow, as he did when solving crosswords. "First, this pranking was at the house of your granny then at your house and then at school."

"And someone has done the prank on us too," added Arvo. "That gold suit of the disco."

Soapy smiled. "But it's all great fun – I've never seen Chinny so mad."

Arvo suddenly went into whisper mode. "Careful, coming this way is Venus."

Venus sauntered over with four of her friends, each a large, sneering girl.

"I bet it's you lot that have been playing tricks on Chinny. I might snitch on you."

Soapy couldn't help answering. "It wasn't us so what's the point?"

"Shut it, Cheeseboy. Still got your cheapo mobile have you?" Two of the girls sniggered, unconvincingly.

"Why do you keep giving us the pester?" said Arvo.

Venus pushed him hard in the chest. "You shut it as well. You can't talk proper and you're not even English. My uncle says you Polish people are ruining our country."

"We're Estonian, not Polish," said Loogi.

Soapy hated it when this happened. He just wanted Venus to go away. He shut the situation out of his mind by continuing the conversation in his head.

*"Why would anyone want to polish people*

*anyway, Venus?"*

*"Yer what?"*

*"You said, 'You polish people'. Is it to make them shiny?"*

*"Polish people, Cheeseboy. I'm talking about Poles."*

*"What kind of poles? Curtain poles? North poles? Magnetic poles?"*

*"Are people from Poland magnetic?"*

*"Only the steel workers."*

Just then the bell went.

After break it was Science. Soapy used to like Science in his last class but with Chinny it was as deadly dull as everything else. One of the reasons that it was so boring was that they never got to do any experiments. Chinny did them all himself and the class just had to watch and write about it afterwards. On this occasion he was demonstrating 'dissolving'. He set up a table next to his desk upon which were four large glass beakers and four jars of powder plus a large plastic bottle. Chinny tapped a metal spoon against the beaker to get everyone's attention.

"Right, clash, watch carefully. We're going to find out which shubstancesh disholve in water. I have here shalt, shand, flour and sugar."

This is going to be exciting, thought Soapy. At least he can say sugar.

Chinny opened the bottle and poured water into one of the large beakers until it was half full. He stopped and wrinkled his nose then leant forward and sniffed the beaker.

"Hmm, right, let's shee what happensh when we shtir in some shalt." Soapy looked across at Arvo who was yawning. The salt dissolved. Soapy wrote in his book 'salt dissolves'.

Next, Chinny filled another beaker with water

and added the sand, which didn't dissolve.

How amazing. Soapy wanted to write that in his book but thought better of it.

Next came the flour.

Except it wasn't flour.

And the water that Chinny poured it into wasn't water, it was clear vinegar.

Of course, this was only discovered afterwards – after the explosion.

Well, it wasn't exactly an explosion but it was spectacular, and Soapy would never forget it. The moment that Chinny dropped the white powder into the beaker there was a great fizzing, boiling commotion and huge white bubbles erupted out of the container, spilling over the sides and onto the table. Chinny yelped and fell backwards. The class stared, transfixed. The bubbling mixture continued to expand and pour out of the beaker like a mini lava flow. It soon covered the table and started dripping onto the floor and then onto Chinny's desk, covering his notes and a pile of essays. Chinny leapt forward and opened his mouth wide to let out a bellow.

Except no bellow came.

Poor Chinny had forgotten his ill-fitting teeth. The moment he opened his gob fully, they slid forward and dropped into the volcano in front of him and were swiftly swallowed by the froth. His eyes expanded and his mouth shrivelled. He suddenly looked very old and frightened. There was a collective gasp and he turned and fled through the door.

Late that evening Soapy was lying on his bed when his mobile beeped with a text from Arvo.

Put your phone on silent. I am needing to call you. This is too important for texting.

A minute later they were talking. Or rather whispering in Soapy's case – his parents would

be furious if they found him still awake, never mind having a phone conversation.

"What's up, Arvo?"

"We have been thinking about all these pranks that are going on."

"Me too – I still can't believe what happened to Chinny. Who would dare to do that?"

"Well, that is exactly what I and Loogi have been wondering. Has there been any more pranking at your house?"

Soapy slid under his duvet. "Well not actually at my house but when my mum got in she starting asking me about our neighbours and she didn't look happy."

"What are you meaning?"

"Well, Mr and Mrs Henderson next door called her at work to say that someone had vandalised their garden. All 61 of their garden gnomes had disappeared in the night and been replaced with Storm Troopers."

"What, real ones?"

"No, those action figures. Anyway, the Hendersons wanted to know if we had heard or seen anything."

"But you would have told us at school if you saw any evidences of this."

"Of course I would. And if I'd known about Old Yorky I'd have told you that too."

"Who is this Old Yorky?"

"He's this grumpy codger who lives across the road. Mr York. He was pranko mucho last night too. He woke up this morning and found himself on the roof of the town hall."

"How is this?"

"He said he fell asleep in his recliner chair and someone must have carried him out in the night and put him on the roof. He had to be rescued by the fire brigade – *and* he was wearing tights and a tutu."

"What is two-two?"

"It's one of those little frilly skirt things that girls put on for ballet. Anyway, he's asked the police to arrest any yobs who have mountaineering equipment."

For a moment there was no answer then Soapy heard the Twince speaking in Estonian before a different voice returned in his ear.

"Loogi here. Arvo has told me all these strange things. But I have a question. Last night, there were no more pranks at your house?"

"No, why?"

"Well, I have made an observation. There is something most strange about these pranks."

Soapy chuckled. "They're all quite strange, I would say – and hilarious too!"

Loogi didn't join in the laughter. "Have you noticed something, though, Soapy? It is like... a kind of pattern."

"What do you mean?"

"Well, think about who has been the prank victim so far: your granny, your mum and dad, Ivette, us, Chinny, and now your neighbours."

Soapy swallowed. "Right, I get it. They're all people connected with me."

"Exactly. We have not heard about anyone

else who has had a big pranking – only people you know."

Once more Soapy heard the brothers pass over the phone and Arvo came back on.

"Soapy, also there is one person who has not been suffering the prank yet, either."

"I know, I was thinking about that earlier: me. I must be next."

"You could be, or maybe there is another way to explain all this," said Arvo with a serious tone. "We are making a theory – but perhaps you will be finding it very strange."

Soapy was sweating under his duvet. "There's something else very strange too. Something I haven't told you yet."

"What is this?"

"Remember the Mini-Bel cheeses that someone put in my bag at Granny's? I went into the shed to check on them this evening. There are two missing."

# 9
# The theory

Soapy slept well that night – better than he had done for days in fact, and he walked with an extra bounce in his step on the way to school with Arvo and Loogi.

"Right you two, let's hear your explanation of the pranks, then. I still don't understand why you couldn't tell me last night."

Arvo looked over his shoulder. "There was too much of the risk."

"And you would not have believed us anyway," added Loogi.

"Why not? What is this theory? You two are driving me nuts."

Arvo patted Soapy on the back. "Don't worry, we will be giving you the big explain."

"Well come on, tell me now."

Loogi shrugged. "We can't – it will take at least half of the hour. We have to be at school in ten minutes."

"Half an hour!"

"Actually, what we are really needing is a whole night." Arvo twiddled a rabbit's thigh bone between his long fingers. "You see, we don't just want to be telling you our theory about the pranks, we want to do the test – to see if it is correct."

Soapy shook his head. "You're like a couple of mad scientists you two…"

Loogi smiled. He liked the idea of being a crazy professor. "Well, I have been following all the clues and adding together the evidences… it just remains for us to carry out the experiment for the proof!"

"I just don't get this," said Soapy. "Where and when can we do this?"

Arvo looked around to see if anyone nearby could overhear them. "We are thinking Saturday night. The best thing would be if we are having a sleepover."

"But sleepovers are for girls. Anyway, my mum won't let me spend the night at friends' houses because of my sleepwalking."

Loogi nodded. "That is OK – your house will be best. Just tell your mum that Estonian boys have sleepovers all the time."

Soapy furrowed his brow. "Right then, Saturday night at my house – but you'd better tell me everything if I've got to wait that long."

They turned into the school gates amidst the sounds of car doors slamming and kids running after footballs.

"One more thing we are liking to know," said Arvo, looking at Soapy. "You've been complaining

of the headaches just recently. Did you wake up with the headache this morning?"

Soapy shook his head. "No, why?"

The Twince nodded at each other. "We didn't think you would."

The rest of the week was uneventful. There were no pranks at the Thompson house and no complaints from the neighbours. Chinny installed new teeth and all seemed to return to normal. Soapy found it quite a relief and soon stopped thinking about Arvo and Loogi's mysterious theory. His parents' mood improved too, and they were reasonably happy for the sleepover to go ahead, even if his mum did hand him a two page printed document of 'Don'ts':

DON'T:
- MAKE A LOT OF NOISE
- JUMP ON THE BEDS
- JUMP ON EACH OTHER
- PLAY DARES
- SPEND ALL NIGHT TALKING ABOUT BODILY FUNCTIONS
- RAP

- SNORT AT RUDE JOKES
- BUILD A TOWEL IGLOO
- TELL GHOST STORIES
- HIT EACH OTHER WITH PILLOWS, BOOKS OR FURNITURE
- DO ANYTHING WITH INK, PAINT, CUSTARD, GLUE, GRAVY, VARNISH, CREAM, SHAMPOO, EGGS OR MARMITE
- TRY AND MAKE AN ELECTRIC GUITAR (LIKE LAST TIME)
- BURP
- RECREATE ANY FAMOUS BATTLES

On Saturday Soapy began to get excited about the night ahead and when the Twince arrived at 8pm the three boys bounded upstairs to Soapy's room clutching bulky bags.

A deep voice boomed from the living room.

"If you're staying up there, lights out by ten. And don't forget your teeth." Soapy smiled to himself. It's always teeth. Why can't parents use more imagination? What about, 'Don't forget your elbows'? Or, 'Don't forget your neck'? When I'm a father it's definitely going to be, 'Don't forget your oesophagus'.

Arvo and Loogi spread out their sleeping bags on the carpet while Soapy put a pile of heavy books in front of the door to discourage what he called 'rapid parental intrusion'.

"Well the pranks seem to have stopped," he said, testing the door.

Loogi nodded. "That is what we were expecting."

"Part of your great theory?"

"Yes, actually."

"This explanation better be good because you two are getting on my nerves. Anyway, there has been one more strange development you don't know about that I need to tell you."

Arvo put a finger to his lips. "Let me be guessing... the Mini-Bel cheeses have vanished."

Soapy squinted. "How did you know that?"

"We took them!" said Loogi. "On Tuesday night after our phone conversation, we sneaked out of our house and broke into your shed."

This is weird. "What! Why?"

Arvo chuckled and pulled the bag of tiny

NOTE: 'Rapid parental intrusion' is a deliberate act of one or both parents to spoil ALL fun.

cheeses from his holdall.
"We have brought them
with us too. But, worry
don't – sit on your bed
and we'll do explaining
what all this is about."

Soapy dived on his
bed and prepared to hear the
Twince unravel their tale. As usual, Arvo
did most of the talking. Loogi meanwhile fiddled
with a crossword from his pocket.

"Ever since we heard about what happened
at your granny's we have been wanting to solve
the mystery of the pranks. We decided to be
using the deduction, like Sherlock Jones."

"And Doctor Watsit, no doubt," added Soapy.

"Watson, actual. But anyway, we have been
noticing something of much interest. Every
person around here has had to suffer the prank
but you. You are the only one who has not had
the pranking. That is very odd."

"So what?"

"Can't you see?" said Loogi.

Arvo was more direct. "We are thinking
it is you!"

Soapy half-laughed. "But it can't be me.
I haven't done any of the pranks. If I had done
them I think I'd know about it."

"But you are forgetting of something. You
sleepwalk." Arvo's voice sounded triumphant.

"Well, yes, I do sleepwalk sometimes, but I
couldn't have sleepwalked all the way to school
to prank Chinny's desk, could I? And are you
saying I sleeprobbed the toy shop to get 61 Storm
Troopers to swap for Mr Henderson's gnomes?"

Arvo put up his hands. "A good point you
are making, so although we think it was you,
we are also thinking that it wasn't you."

"You two have really lost me now." Soapy
slumped onto his bed but Loogi's eyes became
animated.

"You see, as well as Shoelock Holmes, we
have borrowed other books from the library.
Have you heard of Doctor Jekyll and Mr Hyde?"

"They sound like dodgy accountants to me."

"It is the story of the scientist who drinks

a potion and turns into an evil creature with the hunch of the back."

"Sounds a barrel of laughs. Anyway, I've been trying to cut down on secret potions just recently – they give me wind."

Arvo stood up. "Soapy, are you not seeing what has happened? Sleepwalking isn't the only thing you've been doing. What about the eating of cheese?"

"I'm allergic to ch... wait a minute. Are you saying I've been eating ch... like the gorgonzola at Granny's? And the Mini-Bels in the shed? When I've been sleepwalking?"

"Exact," said Loogi.

Soapy gulped. "And when I eat the cheese I turn into a prank-crazed monster?"

He shivered. It's not possible. It can't be. Can it? Is it?

Arvo looked at Loogi. "We've called him Prankenstein."

# 10
# The experiment

Soapy didn't know whether to laugh or cry or sit and think. The Twince wasted no time in detailing the evidence. Loogi showed him some of their notes:

THE INCIDENT OF THE STAIRLIFT
1. THERE WAS GORGONZOLA IN THE FRIDGE
2. THE STAIRLIFT MODIFIED IN THE NIGHT
3. THE BITS OF CHEESE ON THE FLOOR

THE STOOL OF MRS THOMPSON
1. THERE WERE MINI-BEL CHEESES IN THE HOUSE
2. THE STOOL WAS DISCOVERED GLUED TO BUM FIRST THING IN MORNING
3. THE CHEESES WERE IN SOAPY'S BAG

# THE BIG TEETH OF CHINNY
## 1. THERE WERE MINI-BEL CHEESES IN THE SHED
## 2. THE CHINNY TEETH WERE SWAPPED IN THE NIGHT
## 3. ONE OF THE CHEESES WAS MISSING NEXT MORNING.

Soapy was impressed by their careful recording of the facts. "So, the pranks always seem to happen at night and to someone I know."

Loogi nodded. "And there has been access to cheese each time for you."

"So, I could have sleepwalked and done them, I suppose. But what about the last few days – there haven't been any pranks."

Arvo smiled. "That is because there has not been any cheese – we took it from the shed, remember."

It does all seem to fit together... the headaches in the mornings... the types of pranks that I've always dreamed about...

Soapy looked up. "So why have you brought the cheese tonight?" But before they could answer he recalled Loogi's words: "It just remains for us to carry out the experiment".

This could be nasty.

It soon became clear to Soapy that the brothers had thought it through carefully. The only way to prove the theory and find out the truth about Soapy and Prankenstein was to watch him through the night. They produced a huge flask of coffee explaining that this would enable them to keep awake while Soapy slept. They also had a torch, which they would use if they heard him getting up, and their mobile phones ready to film the transformation. Arvo then produced a foil package from his bag, which he carefully unwrapped to reveal four comically thick egg sandwiches.

"What are those for?" said Soapy. "Some special part of the experiment?"

"No, those are for when Loogi is getting hungry. He is always seeking the hoagie."

"Hey, that is not strictly truth," wailed Loogi eyeing the hefty rolls. "Can I have one now?"

Soapy laughed as his friend munched away while flicking through a crumpled book of crosswords he had slipped from a pocket. Arvo had also brought along a newly acquired collection of animal bones to sort to keep himself occupied during the long hours of the night. Soapy wondered why he'd never developed a hobby, unless dreaming of pranks counted, that is.

When the hall clock downstairs bonged for 10pm the Twince placed a Mini-Bel cheese on Soapy's desk and told him to brush his teeth, get into his pyjamas, go to bed and act normally.

"But I've never been normal," said Soapy.

Arvo took a loud slurp of strong Estonian coffee. "True, but you are knowing what we mean."

The experiment had begun.

NOTE: 'Hoagie' is a kind of long monster sandwich shaped like a submarine and much loved by the greedy.

# 11
# An eventful sleepover

Arvo and Loogi sat up against the chest of drawers in Soapy's bedroom in the gloom watching their friend wriggle in his bed. Soapy himself was having trouble getting to sleep – he was simply too excited and scared.

What if I really am Prankenstein?

How will I know I've changed if it happens when I'm asleep?

Will I ever be able to see Prankenstein if I'm him?

Is there going to be bolt through my neck?

The questions rolled round and round in his brain keeping him awake for at least an hour. Arvo, however, soon fell asleep. Loogi nudged him with a sharp elbow.

"Wake up, you panhead – we're supposed

to be watching Soapy."

Arvo's eyes barely opened. He took a sip of lukewarm coffee and mumbled something to his brother. It was no use, Arvo had always been the one who fell asleep instantly. In the

car, on the beach, even at the cinema.

"You are being hopeless," whispered Loogi, watching his brother's eyelids drooping once more.

Another hour passed and finally Soapy was motionless in bed. Arvo was snoring cheerily and Loogi was desperate for the loo.

He had finished most of the giant flask of coffee, knowing that he needed to stay awake to watch his friend. The bathroom was just across the hall but it was just too risky to leave him, even for a moment.

Loogi squeezed his legs together and gritted his teeth. He lasted for ten more minutes then he knew that there was going to be a seriously unpleasant accident if he didn't do something urgently. He reached for the torch and switched it on, being careful to keep the beam off Soapy as he scanned the room for a container.

He crawled towards the door and saw Soapy's school bag. There had to be something in it or he would burst. There was an empty 'XV' Sports drinks bottle. It would have to do – but he would need to put the torch down during the tricky operation. He rested it on the bag and glanced at Soapy's sleeping figure before ripping off the top of the drinks bottle.

The relief was glorious. But in mid-leak Loogi heard a noise behind him. There was a kerfuffle from Soapy's bed but it was impossible to see without the torch and it was also impossible to stop what he was doing – he required two hands. With a superhuman effort he leaned forward and tried to get hold of the torch with his teeth. There was even more noise. He knocked the torch over. Then, finally, he stopped peeing and was able to pick up the torch and turn around.

Soapy was gone.

Not only that, but the Mini-Bel cheese had vanished and the bedroom window was open, its curtain swaying lightly in the night breeze.

Loogi put the lid back on the bottle, gave Arvo a kick on the bum and rushed to the window.

# 12
# The terrible truth

Oh my head.

Soapy sat up with his skull throbbing once more. He looked across the room and saw the Twince sprawled over their sleeping bags on the floor. He tried to piece together what had happened in the night but his brain felt like a lump of porridge – a lump of porridge being hit by a cricket bat. He vaguely recalled trying to get to sleep but that was all.

He slid out of bed and gave Arvo a prod in the back with his big toe.

"Wakey, wakey, Estonia."

It came out as a croak.

Arvo rolled over and stretched, accidentally whacking Loogi on the ear.

"Otch! What for did you do that?" Soapy managed a smile. Did they really say otch instead of ouch?

Arvo sat up and rubbed his eyes. "Sorry, it was the accident, but at least it woke you up. I had a terrible night's sleep – I need a drink – what's in this?" He reached over and picked up the XV Sports bottle.

"Nooo!" screeched Loogi, grabbing it off him. "That is really nasty nasty."

"I have drinked it before. It's not that bad," said Arvo.

"This one is, for sure."

Soapy yawned. "Did anything happen last night then?"

Loogi suddenly remembered why they were there. "You're back!"

"I'm back? I haven't been anywhere."

"Oh yes you have," said Loogi, rubbing his ear.

Then it all came to him, why they were here. The experiment. The cheese. Prankenstein.

"Well what happened? What did you see? Did I sleepwalk? Did I eat the cheese? Did I get up? Did I —"

"Hey, schtoppp." Arvo held up his palm. "If you give us a chance we'll be telling you."

Soapy had now forgotten about his headache and was bouncing on the bed with nervous excitement.

Loogi stood up then sat on the chair by Soapy's desk. "Well, first thing of all, my brother here fell asleep before you did, as the usual, so that part of the plan did not work so well. I drank most of the coffee trying to stay awake but you did eventually fall asleep as well. After the while I heard a noise and I, er, was looking for the torch but could not find it. By the time it was located you were gone."

"Gone where? Out of the door, you mean?"

"No, your outway was the window. Except I think it was not you."

"What do you mean?"

"Well, the cheese was gone, and we saw something when we took the look outside."

Arvo was desperate to join in. "I woke up and we both did rushing to the window. There was much dark but we were clearly observing a figure pass under the lamppost."

Soapy's mouth was dry. "A figure? What sort of figure?"

Loogi looked at his bother then at his friend. "It was short and wide and hairy."

"With the fat fingers and long nails like the claw," added Arvo.

"Well that can't have been me, I'm quite thin and my mum cuts my nails twice a week."

Loogi's eyebrows rose a fraction. "He was wearing the Bart Simpson pyjamas."

Soapy looked down at his chest to see a smiling yellow face and a speech bubble with the words 'Eat my jim-jams.'

The three boys sat in silence for a minute trying to comprehend what had happened. Arvo spoke first. "We were being most stupid not to take the photograph."

Soapy wasn't listening. "So there really is a Prankenstein and it's me?"

"Most true. We were waiting for you to come back but you were gone a long time and we just fell into sleep eventually," said Arvo.

Loogi looked at Soapy who was staring ahead. "Do you not remember anything of this happening then, Soapy?"

Soapy looked at his hands and then felt his neck. "I wonder if I had a bolt?"

"Did you do any of the pranking?" said Arvo.

"Maybe it was just a large nail or a screw."

"Are you listening to us?" said Loogi.

"I wonder if they'll make movies about me?"

"SOAPY!"

"What?"

"Can you remember anything about what you were doing last night?"

"I don't know – I don't remember."

"Do you recall eating the cheese?" said Arvo.

Loogi tutted. "Of course not – he was asleep – well, sleepwalking."

Soapy seemed to wake out of his reverie. "Have you checked the other cheeses?"

They hadn't. Arvo grabbed his bag and shook

it upside down. "They are gone. He must have done scoffing the lot."

"Wait a minute," said Loogi. "You jump to the conclusion. Remember Sherlock Jones. Is there any evidence?"

Soapy looked around. There was a Mini-Bel wrapper on the desk. "He's right, Arvo. There's only one wrapper. If I, er, Prankenstein had eaten them all, there'd be more."

Loogi looked worried. "Do you realise what this means? Prankenstein has hidden the other cheeses. He is able to get them whenever he has the like."

Arvo bumped a hand onto his head. "He will be doing the pranks all of the time, and we will be victims again. Oh no…"

Soapy tried to sound upbeat. "Hey, it's not that

bad is it? Prankenstein might not get you. He might get Chinny again or someone gross like Venus Bray. I'll have a word with him."

"Soapy, it is not so funny. You are the only one who does not have the suffering," said Arvo.

Loogi nodded. "And you have no control over Prankenstein anyway, Soapy. Even you cannot stop him getting us again."

Soapy couldn't really understand why they were so worried. Then a thought hit him.

"Oh no."

"What?" said Arvo.

"Well if Prankenstein keeps getting out and doing worse and worse pranks then sooner or later the Police are bound to catch him – and I will end up in prison. My mum will be really mad then."

For fifteen minutes the three boys swapped ideas about what to do. The Twince agreed that they somehow needed to stop Prankenstein. Arvo twiddled with some adder ribs while Loogi made a list. Soapy didn't like the sound of most of the solutions:

1. TIE S TO HIS BED EACH NIGHT
2. LOCK HIM IN HIS ROOM
3. CALL THE BBC
4. HIRE A BEEFY HENCHMAN TO STOP HIM GETTING OUT
5. LEAVE HIM ON A DESERT ISLAND

Soapy was just about to point out that this was him they were talking about when there was a rapping on the door. Mum.

"Boys, hurry up and get dressed!" She sounded tense. "Arvo and Loogi are being picked up at ten which is in thirteen and a half minutes." There was a pause. "And can any of you explain why there's a cow in the kitchen?"

# 13
# The ultimate prank

The kitchen was bad.

The cow, a large brown and white beast, hadn't actually done any damage but the floor was spectacularly splattered. After the wide-eyed Twince had been taken home, Soapy went in for a closer look. Dad had managed to lure the animal into the back garden where it was happily chewing Mum's begonias. He was now on the phone to the police.

"Yes, of course it's a real cow... No I am not wasting police time. Pardon? You'll be at least forty minutes because there's been a spate of calls this morning about strange incidents? Well, I think finding a cow in your kitchen is pretty damn strange myself. What am I supposed to do with it while I'm

waiting, officer?" His voice then rose a notch.
"No, I do not know how to milk it!"

After looking at the cow in the garden and
wondering where on earth he could have got it
from, Soapy returned to the kitchen. Mum and
Ivette were on their hands and knees scraping
the steaming green muck into carrier bags. Mum
stopped when she saw Soapy in the doorway.

"Was it you who did this, Pugh?"

"No, I always use the toilet."

She didn't seem to appreciate the wisecrack.
"I mean brought that cow in here as a
practical joke?"

"No, it was Pr... probably some of those big kids from the secondary school – they often do cow-based pranks." He suddenly felt hot. Mum stood up and pushed her hands into her back.

"Well, I just hope for your sake, young man, that it wasn't you because if it was you would regret it forever, believe me." Soapy noticed that her lips were thin and tense. "Now come and scrape some of this... dung into a bag. Ugh!"

Back in his room, Soapy flopped onto his bed. He had never seen Mum look so stressed. He needed to think.

Does she suspect something? Well, I was telling the truth. It wasn't me – it was Prankenstein. But what else did I- did he do last night? What if they find out about him? What about the police? I need to find that cheese.

He stood up and wondered where he should start looking. He opened the door then stopped.

Hang on. What am I thinking? Why do I need to stop him? I've always wanted to do pranks. This is my big chance. I can do any pranks I like! And even if they do find out that

I'm Prankenstein it's not my fault. It's his!
I just go to bed each night and fall asleep –
I'm totally innocent!

Soapy began to shiver with excitement at the possibilities. He jumped back on his bed and rolled about.

Just think of the pranks I can do – almost anything...

Crank phone calls
Order a Ferrari
Put a cactus in someone's bed
Pie the Prime Minister.

I'll do the greatest pranks ever seen. I'll invent new, outrageous ones. I'll be able to outprank anybody – I'll be the World Champion, the legendary Prankmeister... and if people get upset then no one can blame me because it won't be me – it'll be Prankenstein!

His mind raced, creating more and more daring japes, tricks and wind ups. And then it came to him: the ultimate prank. He couldn't resist it. He stood up on his bed and shouted it out.

"I'll give the Queen a wedgie!"

A small cough made him spin around quickly. Venus Bray stood in the doorway.

"Shall I tell you how to get to Buckingham Palace?"

Soapy blushed intensely. "Venus! What are you doing here?"

"My mum and dad came round to talk to yours about something boring. They sent me upstairs to see you for some reason." She made an ugly grimace. "Anyway, Cheeseboy, why are you talking to yourself? I always thought you were weird. And what's all that about the Queen?"

Soapy's heart and mind were both racing. "I'm just coming up with an idea for a story. It's, er, homework."

"Eh? We haven't been given a story for homework. There's something going on here." She peered around the room. "I just heard someone let a cow into your house as well, ha. More pranks again... I wonder who's responsible... maybe someone who is talking about wedgies and stuff like that, eh Cheeseboy?"

Before she said another word Soapy jumped up and shut the door in her face. His chest felt like it was about to explode. She knows.

After sitting on his bed for a while and wondering what to do Soapy heard the sound of car doors closing outside. Quietly he crept onto the landing and down the first few stairs. Below in the kitchen he could hear Mum and Dad talking.

"I don't know why we spend so much time with that family, they're so... loud and vulgar," said Soapy's mum.

His father's voice was tense. "I've explained this before. I see Graham all the time at the golf club and he brings a lot of business to the restaurant. He likes to take people there for lunch – I can't just be rude and say we don't want to see them socially."

"I know, I know, but with everything going on I really could do without going round to theirs and watching videos of that girl and her ghastly TV show."

"We could hardly say no, could we?"

"I'd be more interested in seeing her auditions for the West End theatre – what's the show?"

"The Jungle Book."

"Now that's something worth doing because it can lead on to proper theatre work later on. That's how Henry de Vries's son got launched towards the RSC."

Dad laughed. "I can't see Venus Bray in Hamlet. And that girl does far too much of all this show stuff in my view – she's just a kid and it's too much pressure. Anyway, I need to get changed. I've got muck on my trousers."

Soapy heard approaching footsteps and rapidly ducked back into his room.

At least they didn't mention the pranks. But what's this "RSC" they were on about? Really Scary Choirboy? Roast Slug Casserole? Royal Sausage Club? It could be anything.

Soapy didn't feel any better at lunch. For a start, no one had had time to make anything so they just had bread and cold leftovers, and secondly Dad was recounting what the police had told him when they'd arrived to deal with the cow.

'No wonder they were late coming here. Someone's been doing daft things all over town again. For a start there are posters everywhere advertising free chocolate for anyone who can help paint the Mayor's house dayglow orange. Then most of the road signs have been swapped round. Apparently the golf course is now a public dump and the old people's home is a Laser Maze.'

Soapy's mum shook her head. "But who's doing all this? Do the police have any suspects?" Soapy looked down and wondered why Venus hadn't said anything.

"They reckon it's either some kind of a gang, maybe from another town, going round in the night, or it's a local person who's, you know, a bit off his rocker." He pointed to his head.

"They said whoever it was had also tied a string of sausages to the minute hand of the town hall clock and it's been driving all the local dogs mad, especially at half past the hour."

Soapy shifted in his seat, trying not to look guilty.

Ivette stood up to refill the water jug. "I think it's someone from this area. After all, a lot of these pranks have happened to us and people we know."

Soapy felt himself heat up rapidly again. He looked down and thought about going back to his room. He could feel his mum's eyes surveying him.

"Is there any pudding?" he croaked.

"Just fruit," she replied, still watching him with a furrowed brow. "Have a banana if you're still hungry." Soapy was relieved to get up and walk into the kitchen. He picked up a peach and noticed that the 'apples' in the fruit bowl were, in fact tennis balls. He gave the peach a quick rinse then rushed up to his room, his heart still hammering uncomfortably in his chest.

If only I could control Prankenstein. Then I could just prank the people I want to. And what am I going to do about Venus Bray?

His thoughts were interrupted by a bleep from his mobile. It was a text from Arvo.

`You walnut! 'You' went and added an extra bone to my collection. It was in our bedroom when we got back.`

Soapy couldn't see the problem. Surely Prankenstein had done something harmless this time, or kind even. He texted back.

`That doesn't sound so bad to me` (except his mobile typed 'That doesn't soup so bald to me').

Their reply revealed the problem.

`It's a whale bone from the museum. It's five metres long and we can't even lift it. We think they'll probably want it back.`

Oh, I see...

After this Soapy sent another text to the Twince.

There's one more problem. Venus suspects me.

Their reply was brief.

"Oh dear."

As he undressed ready for bed that night, Soapy's mood turned to despair. Maybe being the ultimate prankster in the world wasn't quite as brilliant as he thought. Venus was going to tell people what she knew. And now Mum was on his case as well. He suspected that it wouldn't be that easy to blame it on Prankenstein, either. After all, he *was* Prankenstein.

Maybe I should stop him.

Soapy sat on his bed and pondered.

I can't just go to sleep. Anything could happen, especially now he's hidden those other cheeses.

He considered pushing his bed against the door and locking the window. But what if I sleepwalk again and just move the bed? And if my parents try to come in they'll really suspect that I'm up to something. Oh bottom, bottom, bottom!

As he lay in bed wondering whether to try and stay awake or go to sleep there was a lot more bottom.

# THE ULTIMATE PRANK

# 14
# Ouch!

Sunday started well. Soapy woke up without a headache. Hey, maybe Sunday is Prankenstein's day off!

It didn't take long for it to turn sour, however.

Dad was tipping about half a jar of marmalade onto a piece of toast as Soapy walked into the kitchen in search of breakfast.

"Hey, where did you get marmalade?" said Soapy. "I thought Mum didn't allow it."

"I have a secret stash in my briefcase. You can have a bit if you don't let on." Dad stuffed the toast into his mouth and stood up. "I'm off to golf in a minute – have you remembered that we're going to the Brays when I get back this afternoon?"

Soapy hadn't. He suddenly didn't feel like

eating anything. His shoulders dropped to somewhere near his waist. "Do I have to go?"

"Course you do – they've invited us round especially to see the new video of Venus doing her song. She's got to the final of Stars of Tomorrow."

"I know, I know." Everybody in the world knows.

Even if Venus didn't live there, Soapy would have hated going to the Brays. They were just so, well, loud. And they were always showing off and talking about money and their latest this and latest that. At least he understood now how his parents ended up as their friends.

But Venus being there was just the end. She gave Mum and Dad huge smiles as they walked through the door.

"Hi Mr and Mrs T! Really pleased you could come." Soapy saw her curl up her lip at him as he reluctantly followed on in. Mrs Bray then screeched and pretended to kiss Mum and Dad as if they had just scored at Wembley.

"Come in, come in, come in!"

She was wearing the most sparkly top

that he had ever seen and had so much make up that she didn't look human at all. Soapy waited nervously as she came over to him and bent down to touch him on the nose in that annoying way that adults do.

Mr Bray ignored Soapy and insisted on pouring Dad a whisky even though it was Sunday afternoon and he was driving. "Siddown while Vee gets the DVD sorted."

He calls her Vee?

"How are The Jungle Book auditions going?" asked Mum.

Mrs Bray fluttered her false eyelashes. "Well, she's made it through two rounds, haven't you, sweetie?"

"Everyone there is very talented so it's difficult," said Venus, "and there's lots of waiting, but they said I have a great voice."

"You must be worn out with doing that and the TV Show," said Dad.

"Well, there is a lot of travelling to London." She glanced at Mrs Bray, who smiled nervously, then pointed the remote control at the gigantic TV on the wall.

Soapy hated the way Venus always sounded so charming when speaking to adults. If only they knew what she was really like. He sank into the white leather settee and wondered how he was going to survive the next hour. The huge screen came to life and there was Venus, almost life-size, standing on a stage wearing a forced grin and a silver dress. The real Venus looked at the screen and took a bow.

Please... one is bad enough.

"My name is Venus Bray and I'm going to sing 'Super Trouper' by ABBA," said the silver Venus. Before she started Mr Bray paused the DVD and made sure Soapy's family knew all the things that they had already been told by Mrs Bray.

"Over sixty five thousand children entered Stars of Tomorrow and Vee's made it to the final eight – not bad for an eleven year-old. We took this video of her final rehearsal at the drama studio in town. She's having her hair and face professionally done for the TV show, of course, and she'll probably wear a gold suit on the night too."

"And I'm going to meet Dijon Sparkes," added Venus. "She's beautiful – my favourite presenter."

Soapy had never heard of her. Mr Bray waited until Dad and Mum had made sufficient cooing noises and then started to play the video. Soapy could see right away that Venus had inherited her parent's volume as she belted out the song and flung her arms about.

If this made the final what were the rejects like? Soapy slumped and waited.

At the end his parents applauded, although he knew that his mum loathed this kind of music, and Dad nudged him to join in. Venus drank it up. Then Mrs Bray turned to him.

"Do you like performing Soapy? Of course, Venus has been winning trophies for singing and dancing since she was three."

"Not really, no."

"That's a shame, but I suppose not everyone can be a star like our daughter, eh?" She winked a horrible wink. Soapy looked at her dyed blonde hair and purple lipstick and couldn't help himself from continuing the conversation in his head.

*Soapy: Star? Venus is a planet, actually.*

*Mrs Bray: I know – we nearly called her Uranus.*

*Soapy: Well she belongs in outer space, for sure.*

*Mrs Bray: Make sure you tell all your friends to vote when she's on telly, won't you?*

*Soapy: Oh, we'll all vote all right…*

"Pugh!"

"Wha- oh, sorry, Mum"

"Didn't you hear what was just said?"

"Er, no."

Mr Bray was rolling his eyes. "I said we're going to have some grown up chat now which will be very boring for you kids so Vee is going to show you her room, aren't you Vee?" Venus didn't answer

but stomped out of the
room
and up the stairs, with
a sour face.

"Well, go on Soapy,
off you go," said Dad.

But she's a bully and
she hates me and she
knows that I'm doing
all the pranks. Soapy
took as long as he dared to get up and
slouched towards the door.

He thought about just sitting on the stairs
but they would think that he was listening
in if they found him. He dragged his feet up
the steps but, despite his slow motion ascent,
the landing came all too soon.

It was obvious which was her room. There
was a huge pink letter V on the door and lots
of glittery stars. It was closed. Soapy decided
to go and sit in the bathroom when the door
opened and Venus stuck her head out.

"There's no way you're coming in my room,

130

Cheeseboy."

"You're right about that."

"And you won't even be going anywhere soon, will you?"

"What do you mean?"

"You're gunna be locked up in one of those young offenders places, like a jail."

"What are you talking about?" Soapy knew perfectly well.

"I mean, you dur, that I know it's you doing those pranks around the town."

Soapy gulped, trying not to show it. "How could it be me?"

"I don't know that yet but I'm going to find out, and then I'm going to choose the right time to tell everyone, and that'll be it for you, Cheesy Thompson."

"What have you got against me, anyway?"

"You think you're clever and I know you hate my singing but I don't care because I'm going to be a star."

"I've never said I hate your singing."

"Huh, I remember when your family came

round here once and I did a song and you didn't clap or anything."

Soapy shook his head. "What? I was about six!"

"You're just jealous."

Soapy had heard enough and started to turn away.

"Hang on, I've got something for you," said Venus.

"What?"

"It's this." She stepped forward and brought a hand from behind her back. Before Soapy realised what was happening she sprayed him in the face with a bottle of perfume. It bit into his eyes and made him jolt back violently into a wall. Before he could say anything, she disappeared into her room again and slammed the door.

His breath was wheezy and he could barely see. His elbow was pulsing painfully too. Groping his way to the bathroom, Soapy found the basin and splashed some water in his eyes. After a minute the tears cleared and he could see, but his chest was still gasping and the

sickly smell of flowery scent was overwhelming.
He sat on the loo and tried to calm himself
and take his mind off the various murderous
threats which his brain was now computing.

The calm lasted about five seconds. That
was when Venus put on 'Super Trouper' at
a booming volume.

She is evil.

He took off his top and washed his face,
neck and arms with soap, scrubbing them as
hard as he could. He hated using other people's
towels, especially ones Venus Bray might have
touched but he dried himself and opened
a window. The smell was still there.

The car journey home turned out to be as
grim as the rest of the afternoon.

"What is that awful stink?" said Dad,
turning around.

Mum glowered at Soapy. "Were you messing
around with Venus's perfume, or her mother's?"

"I don't know whose stupid perfume it was
but she sprayed me in the face with it."

"Well, you must have done something to

provoke her."

"I didn't do anything."

Dad opened a window. "I have to say she is a bit, er, abrasive."

Mum stared at him. "Oh, come on. She wouldn't have done it for nothing."

"She just hates me, that's all," said Soapy.

Mum adjusted her visor mirror so that she could see Soapy without turning round. "There must be more to it than that. Did you say something unkind about her singing?"

"No."

"Are you jealous, young man?"

Not that again. "Never in a million billion willion gillion fillion years am I jealous of Venus Bray!"

Whoops, that was a bit loud.

"Stop the car at once!" screeched Mum. Dad indicated left and stopped at the side of the road. Mum unfastened her seatbelt and turned around. Her face had that dangerous kind of Alex Ferguson look.

"Right, it's time for a talk with you."

Dad looked at her. "I thought we were going to get home first."

"I'm not having him shouting at us in the car." She then turned back to Soapy. "I think you have a real cheek saying that about Venus. Those songs might not be everybody's cup of tea but at least she's achieved something there. And if she gets through the theatre auditions she could be in a proper West End Musical. I wish you would accomplish something. You don't seem to be interested in anything."

Soapy opened his mouth to speak but his disbelief stole the words away. Dad filled the gap. "We've been worried about your behaviour lately too. You've been acting in an odd way over the last week. I know all these strange goings on couldn't be all your doing but we can't escape the feeling that you must be involved somehow."

Soapy didn't know what to say to that one. At least Dad wasn't angry like Mum.

She jabbed her finger. "It's not good enough. I phoned school and talked to your teacher on Friday. He says your work is not always up to the standard expected. I don't know whether it's the friends you hang about with or that you're not being pushed enough but if things don't improve soon then we're going to do some pushing."

"What do you mean?" At least some words came.

Mum looked at Dad, who squirmed slightly, then at Soapy. "Mr Eckersleight told us that auditions are starting next week for the school play."

Soapy was confused. "You mean the show we're doing, Oliver!?"

"Yes, no doubt Venus will have a starring role."

"But, what's that got to do with anything?"

Dad opened another window. "That perfume is gassing me..."

Mum carried on. "I'll tell you what it's got to do with anything. We want you to get a part in that play. And not back row of the choir or fourth urchin – a proper leading role. I know it's a musical but at least it's Dickens. We're sick of hearing from other parents what

their kids are achieving. You don't seem very interested in sport so we want you to get up on that stage and show people what you're capable of – it'll do you good."

"But what if I don't get the part? It's up to the teachers – they might choose someone else."

Dad was about to answer when Mum cut him off. "Like I said – you push yourself. If you don't get it, then we're thinking about sending you to boarding school."

# 15
# Windpipe salad

Soapy decided that he knew seven things about boarding school:

1. They flush your head down the toilet. In fact bogwashing happens daily.
2. The school dinners are things like windpipe salad and lungs á l'orange.
3 You have to play rugby against hulking bruisers who are encouraged to crack bones and spill blood.
4. Each day begins with a sharp caning, 'to build character'.
5. The only subjects are Latin and Algebra.
6. Everyone wears a top hat and cravat (whatever that it is)
7. The teachers must be called 'Sir master' or they dangle you by the lip.

He wasn't absolutely sure about number five but the rest were undoubtedly true. As he lay on his bed Soapy pondered the horror of life amongst hoards of posh kids.

They can't seriously be thinking of sending me there. Can they?

He then realised that he didn't even know where the nearest boarding school was. There was a private school just outside town. Was that the same thing? And what did 'boarding' mean? Maybe they let the kids have skateboards at break. He decided to Google the word just to see. There was lots about getting on planes and trains. Blimey! The school must be really posh to have its own plane. He googled 'boarding school' just to be sure.

What? WHAT!

He read the words again just to be sure.

A boarding school is an educational institution where some or all pupils not only study, but also live.

Live? Actually sleep at school? But when would he get to see Arvo and Loogi? And then the full horror hit him.

Sleeping at school.

Sleepwalking.

Prankenstein.

There was bound to be cheese in the school. And the pranking opportunities would be immense. And he was certain to be caught.

Soapy scrabbled around for his mobile and texted the Twince. They immediately understood the peril of the situation. As usual, they came up with a plan.

`Right, you've got to do two things:`

`1. Get a part in the play`

`2. Stop Prankenstein from the ruining of your chances - find those Mini-Bels!`

They were right. If he could stop Prankenstein, at least over the next few days, his parents might be less suspicious and he could concentrate on the auditions at school. Soapy looked at his watch. 7.22pm. There were still a couple of hours of daylight. The Mini-Bels couldn't be far – Prankenstein would have hidden them where Soapy could reach them easily when sleepwalking. Searching his bedroom would be simple but the other rooms presented a bit more of a problem, with Mum, Dad and Ivette all at home. It had to be done, though.

Forty minutes later Soapy flopped back down on his bed. He'd searched every drawer, cupboard, space, box, shelf and bag in his room. He'd emptied the wardrobe and lifted every book out of his bookcase. He'd taken his bed apart and prodded the mattress but there was nothing. The bathroom was clear too. He wondered about the kitchen next – he could pretend he was getting a snack, but it was still risky.

Come on, come on.

Then, much to Soapy's surprise, his brain began to engage.

Hang on, hiding them in the kitchen doesn't make sense. Mum or Dad or Ivette could easily find them. The same applies to the living room and dining room. He's crafty so he's more likely to have put them in the garden or somewhere nearby outside.

Soapy looked out of his window. It was a bit of a drop down to the garage roof but the drainpipe would help. At least he could get out without being noticed. Anyway, this was Prankenstein's exit and if Soapy was to beat him then he had to use the same advantages. He swung the window fully open and stepped onto the ledge.

It was only when he scrambled to the ground with his heart fluttering that a question occurred to him.

How am I going to get back in?

Jumping down was definitely easier than climbing up. He would just have to check that his parents were in the living room then he could sneak in through the back door and tiptoe up the stairs. Ivette was bound to be in her room on the phone to her boyfriend.

Soapy looked at the large back garden with

its shrubs, compost heaps, hedges, great bushy flowers, trees and shed and realised just how many places there were to hide a bag of small round cheeses. Searching would take hours.

Wait a minute.

Shed.

They couldn't be. Could they?

Soapy sneaked down to the shed, sure that mistrustful neighbours were eyeing him. It was unlocked, as usual. Mind you, it was only full of old tat now that Dad kept his power tools in the garage. The plant pots were still there. He lifted the large one where he'd first hidden the cheeses himself, what seemed like weeks ago.

And there they were, four little round red Mini-Bels in a bag.

One-nil!

Maybe Prankenstein's not so clever after all.

He stuffed them under his t-shirt and crept out of the shed, heading towards the back door. Then he stopped. In his excitement he'd completely forgotten what he needed to do next.

Why am I taking them into the house? I need

to get rid of them!

He sat down behind the shed and considered his options. He'd never really had to destroy cheese before. What was the best way? Burn it, probably. But how would he do that?

He could bury it in the soil. No, it could be dug up.

Hit it with a spade? Stupid.

Throw it over the fence into next door's? Dur…

The more he thought about it, the more he realised that getting rid of cheese was not by any means as easy as it sounded. Were there any websites on the subject? Books? Forums? www.how-to-lose-cheese.com maybe? Perhaps there was a helpline he could ring? His mind inevitably began to drift.

*Soapy: Hello, is that the Emergency Cheese Destruction Service?*

*ECDS agent: Yes sir, may I help you?*

*Soapy: I am in possession of four live Edams. I need help.*

*ECDS agent: Right sir, first thing is I need you to do is remain calm. Please do not touch the cheeses. Have you got that?*

*Soapy: Understood. What should I do?*

*ECDS agent: First of all, sir, I need you to place the cheeses down upon a hard surface, but do it very gently. Then I want you to withdraw slowly to a distance of at least twenty metres. Those babies could go off at any moment.*

*Soapy: Then what happens?*

*ECDS agent: I've already radioed the nearest Cheese Disposal Squad. They'll be with you within eleven minutes. Stay calm.*

*Soapy: Thank you.*

*ECDS agent: You're welcome – but sir, please do not be tempted to return to the cheeses or to touch them. We have sophisticated machinery to take care of them. Your worries are over.*

A cat screeching from a nearby garden brought Soapy back to his senses. He stood up and decided to throw the Mini-Bels into the boating lake at the park.

He ran there and back without stopping and was more than relieved to discover that the cheeses didn't float. He didn't think anyone had seen him but even if they had, a boy lobbing a few small red things into a pond wasn't going to arouse a great deal of attention after the havoc wrought by Prankenstein.

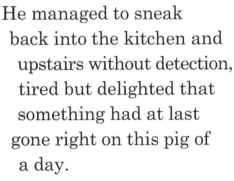

He managed to sneak back into the kitchen and upstairs without detection, tired but delighted that something had at last gone right on this pig of a day.

As it happened, nobody had seen Soapy throw the cheeses into the lake. But nor had Soapy noticed the local newspaper on a rack by the door of Late Stop Shop as he sprinted past. The headline said 'More on Local Prank Spree' and at the bottom was a small paragraph stating that The Epicure Delicatessen in Goat Lane had reported an unusual robbery. 5kg of best Stilton had been stolen on Friday night.

NOTE: 'Stilton' is a cheese that's even stinkier than Gorgonzola.

# 16
# More please

Mr Eckersleight scratched his wig and looked at the assembled children.

"Well, we seem to have rather a lot of volunteers for parts in the school play this year, which is good in a way, although it means many of you will be disappointed, of course."

Soapy shifted uneasily in his chair and looked around. There were about twenty five juniors in the classroom for the lunchtime auditions and he knew from the announcement in assembly that there were only seven main parts. Still, he was glad to see Arvo and Loogi there to give him support.

"Right, we'd better make a start," said Mr Eckersleight, reaching for a pile of papers. "I've brought along some scripts for Oliver!, which is a musical, as you know. It's based on one of Charles Dickens' stories."

"Which one?" said Arvo.

Soapy was eager to get noticed. "Was it A City of Two Tales, Mr E?"

"Don't be fool," said Loogi, before Mr Eckersleight could react. "There is no such book. My father is a big Dickens fan. It is A Tale of Two Cities."

"No it's not," said Mr Eckersleight.

Arvo put up a finger. "Then maybe A Tale of Three Cities?"

Soapy saw Mr E shaking his head. "Er, is it David C..."

"David Kipperfield?" said Arvo, trying to help his friend. Several children laughed.

"Not that one," said Loogi, seeing Mr E

chuckling too. "Then maybe Great Ex..." with his eyes he urged Soapy to complete the title.

"Oh yes, Great, er, Excuses."

Seeing Mr E sighing he tried again. "Great Expenses?"

Arvo decided to join in. "Great Extensions?"

Soapy thought hard. "Great Explosions!"

"No boys, it is not based on Great Expectations," said Mr E.

"Then maybe it is being that knickerless boy?" said Arvo.

"You are meaning Nicholas Nickleby," said Loogi in despair.

"It's based on Oliver Twist, you berks." It was Venus Bray. Soapy hadn't noticed that she'd just come in. He tutted inwardly as she walked straight to the front and sat next to the Headteacher, wearing a smug expression. "Don't you remember, Mr Eckersleight, I was the star of the show when we did 'A Christmas Carol' – but then I have seen 'Scrooge' in London six times."

Mr Eskersleight nodded. "Oh that's right. You were very good, Venus – it was such a pity that the Ghost of Christmas Past was sick on Tiny Tim."

"I hope I'm going to have a big part in this play too," Venus flashed her false smile.

"You could be the baddie Fagin – you've got the right personality," said Soapy, immediately wishing he could unsay it as she shot him a venomous glance.

Mr Eckersleight nodded at Venus. "I'm sure we'll find you something – Nancy perhaps, but I'd like to sort out the part of Oliver first and that really needs to be a boy."

Venus folded her arms and looked away. Soapy sat up and gulped quietly.

"If you remember the story," said Mr Eckersleight, "Oliver is an orphan who lives in the workhouse where he gets into trouble by asking for more gruel. He runs away and joins a gang of pickpocket boys ruled over by the devious criminal Fagin."

Arvo whispered to Loogi, "We are going for something light of the heart, then."

Soapy tried to look serious as he put up his

hand. "I'd like to audition for Oliver please, Mr E."

"Well, I'm very glad you're so keen. Alright then, there's a script here I've written myself as the original is rather too long. Let's try you out on a few lines from Scene One, after the song 'Food Glorious Food'. I'll be Mr Bumble, who's in charge of the workhouse, and you read Oliver's lines up to the end of the first page."

Soapy tried to blank out the idea of Mr E serving thin, lumpy porridge and stood up clutching the script. The Head cleared his throat and went for a weird crone voice:

Oliver: Please sir, I'd like some more.

Mr Bumble: More, did you say?

Oliver: Yes, more.

Mr Bumble: More what?

Oliver: More gruel.

Mr Bumble: Whaaat! Do you think we are made of gruel, boy? Gruel is not free! Gruel costs money, hard cash. We give you enough to keep you alive and that is all you need, impudent youth!

---

NOTE: 'Gruel' is a most disgusting thick, lumpy, sometimes green goo that orphans used to eat in the old days.

Oliver: So, that's a no, then?

Mr Bumble: Take this boy away to be taught a lesson!

Soapy was concentrating furiously on the script but, even though he knew his future depended on winning the part, he simply couldn't stop his mind from wandering.

*This is rubbish. I can't do this.*

Mr Eckersleight stopped and looked at his watch. "Well, that wasn't bad at all, but I think I should try out a few more people. Who else wants to have a go at Oliver?" Eleven arms went up. Soapy groaned. Ben Goodge was selected and once more Mr E launched into his high-pitched Bumble voice.

*I can't listen to this eleven more times, especially as there's bound to be someone better than me.* He decided to pass the time by imagining his own version of Scene One.

*Oliver: I'd like some more please.*

*Mr Bumble: More what?*

*Oliver: Right, I think we'll start with a slice of pepperoni pizza plus a bowl of cheesy nachos with a blueberry shake to wash that down.*

*Mr Bumble: Do you want fries with that?*

*Oliver: Go on then, it's been all go here in the workhouse.*

*Mr Bumble: Sorry sir, we're out of pizza –*
*I can do you a gruel burger or a tripe toastie.*

*Oliver: Forget it, I'm going out for fish and chips. This workhouse is a disgrace.*

Soapy was woken out of his daydreaming by the sound of laughter. Mr Eckersleight wasn't laughing and nor was Ben Goodge, who was frowning. The watching kids were all smiling and looking at each other, however. Mr E chose to ignore the commotion and moved onto the next volunteer. Soapy decided to watch.

This time it was Sanjay Shah's turn to be Oliver. He was going OK until he had to say 'More gruel,' at which point he started to giggle and then splutter, ending up saying 'Gore mule,' which caused uproar.

Mr E flapped his script. "What's got into you all? I said it's a light-hearted show but it's not that funny. Now come on, pull yourselves together. Let's have the next person."

When the fourth volunteer, Harvey Burton, collapsed into snorting sniggers too, Soapy realised what was happening. The Twince had cleverly positioned themselves opposite each boy who was auditioning and behind Me E's back. They waited until the reading started and then they began their own little show. Arvo had stuck two turtle bones up his nostrils. He hid behind Loogi then waited for the right moment. With wide rolling eyes he popped his head out and swayed about in view of the poor performer, making the bones waggle by pulling faces. This happened several times with the same result. The boy would try with all his might not to look at Arvo but it was no use. Each one was rendered helpless. Even Venus was laughing. The head decided that his portrayal of Mr Bumble must be just too hilarious for the children to contain themselves and so moved on to another part.

The following day Soapy arrived at school early. He raced inside and went straight to the noticeboard. There was a sheet of paper listing who had been given the various parts in the show.

He saw that Venus Bray was Nancy and that Arvo and Loogi were pickpockets and that Pugh Thompson was Oliver.

Pugh Thompson – that's you, you fool. You've done it!

The rest of the day passed in a kind of floaty fog as Soapy sat with a dim grin on his face. Even a severe telling off from Chinny couldn't stifle his contentment. He thanked the Twince for their brilliance and looked forward to a life free of bogwashing.

Back at home that evening his mum and dad were almost as pleased as he was. Granny was there visiting too, having just about recovered from her stairlift trauma. Hearing Soapy's news, she was full of questions.

"You're in a play, are you?"

"Yes, we're doing a musical."

"Which part have you got?"

"I'm Oliver."

"I thought you were Pugh."

'No, I mean I play Oliver in the show."

"What is the show?"

"Oliver."

"Now you're calling me Oliver. I'm yer granny, daft boy."

"Er, I'm going to be an orphan."

"Oh dear, your mother and father were only here a moment ago. Nasty accident, was it?"

"No, oh, never mind, Granny."

She chuckled. "You used to look like Winston Churchill when you were a baby, you know."

Helllp!

Soapy arrived for the first rehearsal
along with the Twince who, for once were
in a bad mood. From the start, they argued
continuously about who should be The Artful
Dodger, the chief among the pickpockets.

"I am being older than you, brother, so I should
be the leader of the naughty gang," said Arvo.

"Hah, you were born three minutes before,
that does not really count. Anyhows, the Artful
Dodger sings much in the show but you have
the voice of a chesty rook," replied Loogi.
"I, on other hand, have the voice of Pelvis."

Soapy laughed. "You mean Elvis?"

Arvo waved his arms. "Elvis, Pelvis, what
is it mattering? Loogi you do not even know
what a pickpocket is."

"Pah, of course. It is a thief who steals
people's pockets."

"Steals *from* their pockets, actually," said
Soapy, still laughing.

Loogi folded his arms. "Alright then clever
of the clogs, Arvo. What does 'Artful Dodger'
mean if you know so much?"

"Ah, dodger means he is not being easy
to catch, and, er, artful means, er, he is liking
paintings and sculpture. Maybe."

Loogi stood up smiling in triumph. "Ha,
now is the truth out! Arvo, that is big rubbish.
Artful means clever or tricksy, is that not
correct, Mr E?"

The headmaster, who had been sorting
through a pile of scripts, looked upwards.
"Boys, this is really wasting a lot of time.
Yes, Loogi is right and if he can sing better,
then I suppose he'd better play the Artful Dodger.
Arvo, you can be Charlie Bates – he's the second
main pickpocket so still an important character."

Loogi wore a broad grin while Arvo skulked
towards a corner, with Soapy following to
try and cheer him up. Mr Eckersleight finally
handed out the scripts and walked to the front
of the room. Venus Bray's hand went up.

"Mr E – I do like your tie, by the way – can
we do 'Oom-Pah-Pah' today?"

"What's that?" laughed Soapy, "sounds
like a back to front cow."

Seeing the disgust on Venus's face, Mr E held up his hand. "It's a song from the show, actually. But it doesn't appear till half way through, Venus, so I think we should start at the beginning. Anyway, you must be under strain with all the theatre and TV auditions so have a rest."

Soapy smiled, but Venus shot him a cutting glance and whispered something towards him which looked from her lips like, "I can tell him about you any time."

Soapy kept quiet for the rest of the rehearsal.

On the walk home from school that afternoon with the Twince, Soapy didn't feel like talking.

"What is the matter? You are unusually silent," said Arvo.

Loogi added, "Your acting of Oliver was good, Soapy. You should be pleased."

"I suppose so but I've got loads of lines to learn."

"Come," said Arvo. "Your parents will have big happiness when they see you on the school stage, and then you will not have to be going to that stupid school of the posh."

"It might never happen, though," sighed Soapy.

Loogi put up a finger. "Ah, you are worrying about Venus Bray. Am I right?"

Soapy nodded. "She knows my secret, and she could tell people any time. In fact, I don't know why she hasn't told Mr E or her parents already."

"Ah yes," said Arvo. "But she only suspects you are the king of prank. She is not having the proof."

"No, but if she spills the beans then my parents are going to spy on me all the time and they are bound to discover the truth."

Arvo shook his head. "There is no need for worry. Remember you have killed Prankenstein by the denial of cheese. You threw it in the lake."

"For once, my brother is right," said Loogi. "No cheese, no pranks, no proof, no problem."

"Do you really think Prankenstein's dead, then?" said Soapy.

"This is a question most interesting," said Arvo. "Maybe he is more like hyper nation than actual goner."

"Hibernation," said Soapy, for once not smiling.

Loogi put away the crossword he had been studying and slowed his walk. "This is an important moment I think. Just because Prankenstein has not made a recent appearance he is not gone forever."

"We must be vigilant against cheese access," said Arvo, nodding.

"I know this sounds stupid," said Soapy, "but I kind of miss him. There haven't been any pranks for a while and well, it's a bit boring now. Maybe when the musical is over I could let him have a little run out."

Loogi's mouth was open. "Whaaat?"

"If only I could control him," said Soapy, not seeming to hear him.

Arvo stopped walking. "Are you being the crazy man? Prankenstein is uncontrollable,

that is the whole point. He's… wild, a monster. Remember, we have seen him."

Loogi put a hand on his friend's shoulder. "He is your dark side, Soapy – you can never have control of him because when you are him you are not you."

Arvo nodded. "He's being out of control – just think what he has already done. And remember Venus. You might be giving her the proof."

"Then it would be the private bored school and daily washbogging of the head," added Loogi. "We would lose a good friend too."

Soapy sighed. "As usual you're right. It's just too dangerous – Prankenstein is OTT and I can't let him spoil things now I've got the Oliver part and finally done something right for my parents.

It's a shame, though."

# 17
# Oliver vs Prankenstein

There followed two weeks of intense rehearsing. Soapy's mum helped him to learn his lines and Mr E seemed pleased with his performance as Oliver through each practice. The Headteacher had decided to play the part of the Pickpockets' sneaky leader Fagin himself, claiming that none of the children looked old enough, but Soapy thought that he just wanted to show off on stage.

The Twince and Soapy watched Venus during each rehearsal, waiting for her to say something but the moment never arrived. Soapy wondered whether she was biding her time for a particular occasion when she could do the most damage. It made him feel sick to think of it.

On the other hand, Soapy told himself that Prankenstein was now out of the picture, unable to find the cheese he needed. The pranks had stopped and everybody had stopped talking about them. Maybe Venus had forgotten.

At home, Soapy's parents' mood had improved too and they appeared genuinely excited about their son taking the star role in the school's forthcoming musical.

"Are you going to invite Granny to come along and watch the show?" asked Soapy at the dinner table one night.

"Well, I think we should but your mother disagrees," said Dad.

"She's bound to ruin it by asking loud questions or making other noises – you know what she's like," said Mum. "I couldn't bear

the embarrassment."

"But I'm sure she'd enjoy it," said Soapy, who occasionally liked to stir things at home.

Dad nodded. "Yes, she'd love to see her favourite grandson play Oliver."

"Oh come on," said Mum, shaking her head. "You know perfectly well she's confused about everything and probably wouldn't understand the plot. I mean, it was only last month that she called the police because she ran out of eggs."

Soapy knew it was no use arguing even though Granny would miss out, but from his frustration, deep inside, there arose a thought that was unimaginably dangerous. The temptation to unleash Prankenstein just to teach his mum a lesson.

A few days later there was a flutter of excitement in assembly as Mr Eckersleight asked for quiet.

"That's it, calm down everyone, and please take that ridiculous thing off your head, Rebecca Poskitt. Oh, sorry dear, I didn't realise it's your hair. Now, it's the school production of Oliver! tonight and I just want to underline to everyone how important it is." Soapy looked sideways at Arvo and Loogi while Mr E continued.

"I am particularly glad that all of the recent pranks have stopped because I would have to stop the play and send all of the audience home if one happened this evening during the performance."

"This is our turn to show the parents and governors what we can do as a school and I'm not having it ruined and the staff being made to look fools."

Soapy was thinking that was odd because they normally looked like fools – well, Chinny did, anyway, but he didn't smile at his own wit because he had a slight headache. It had filled him with dread when he'd woken up that morning even though it did at least feel different from his previous Prankenstein headaches. He decided to blame it on nerves due to the closeness of his big night.

Mum and Dad looked cringingly proud as

they drove Soapy to the school that evening.
They'd set off extra early because Dad had
wanted to bag a front-row seat in the hall
so that he could video the show.

"But people with camcorders always stand
at the back, so they can get the whole stage
in the shot," said Soapy.

"I know that, but I'm not interested in
the whole stage – I just want to record you."

Mum interjected before Soapy could say
anything. "Now just focus on your lines, Pugh,
and project every word clearly. You need to
develop a classical acting style from the start.
Just think, this could be the first step towards
The Royal Shakespeare Company."

Oh that's what RSC is...

She turned and looked him over. "Don't
disappear before I've brushed your hair. And
don't stand too near the edge of the stage –
I don't want you falling off."

Soapy half nodded and turned to look out
of the window.

Oh what have I let myself in for?

At seven o'clock the school hall reached its physical capacity. Every chair was taken and there were parents, aunties, uncles, grannies, big sisters, little brothers, cousins, friends and grandads taking up every inch of space. Some were kneeling on the PE benches at the back and a whole line stood up in front of the curtains, each one either perusing a programme, looking for friends or aiming a camera at the stage to test a zoom lens.

Soapy's mum and dad were there on the front row and Mr and Mrs Bray were three seats along from them. The Twince' dad, Olof, was just behind them, next to their mum, Pinja who was holding up their baby brother Mikk.

The teachers meanwhile were all standing in Soapy's classroom and fussing around the cast who were lined up in costumes waiting to go in along with the children who made up the choir. Each one, adult and child, felt a tingly-sickly quiver inside, wondering if it was going to go right and if anyone would remember their lines.

A hairy-faced, scruffily-costumed Mr Eckersleight scurried into the room. It was very strange to see him dressed up as the crafty criminal Fagin.

"Right everyone, remember the opening scene is the workhouse with the orphan boys including Oliver, and even though you might be excited with all the parents in the hall and the cameras flashing try to look miserable and hungry and Victorian – this is a play after all and you need to act.' He looked around with a slight air of panic. 'Where is Mr Bumble? He should be at the front of the line."

"He's gone to the toilet," said Venus Bray, who was in a grouch because she didn't feature in the opening part of the show. Mr E closed his eyes for a moment before the rotund and sweaty figure of Julian Moffat, the boy playing Mr Bumble, appeared in a tweed suit which was tightly fitted over nine jumpers.

"Sorry," he whimpered, barely able to breathe under all the layers designed to make him look chubby.

Mr E held up a hand. "At least you're here now. Julian, do remember that Mr Bumble is the nasty man in charge of the workhouse so give out the gruel with a bit of venom, not that vacant grin please." Julian nodded then the Headteacher scuttled past the line of waiting singers and into the hall before announcing to the crammed audience that the show was now ready to begin. Chinny sat at the piano and played a few introductory bars. Another teacher swung the door open and ushered the choir in.

Soapy gulped then followed Mr Bumble and the scruffy workhouse boys through and

up onto the stage while the spectators clapped manically. He now had a nerve-crunching two minutes on stage joining in the opening song, 'Food Glorious Food'. He didn't dare look at the parents so instead cast his eye over the set, checking that all the props were in place.

The dining benches and bowls and spoons were there, as was the table at the side where Mr Bumble and the cook dished out the orphans' slop from a giant black pot. Soapy didn't want the song to end because that meant that he would have to speak with every eye in the hall watching.

When the song did finish Soapy was surprised when the audience burst into more applause. It gave him just a moment to gather his thoughts as he picked up his bowl and edged across the stage to ask Mr Bumble for more gruel.

"More?!" screeched Julian Moffat in reply to Soapy's request. The audience giggled. 'MORE?' They laughed. Perhaps this wasn't going to be so bad after all.

Soapy put on an extra miserable face as Mr Bumble then announced that he was going to sell Oliver, and while Julian Moffat sang 'Boy for Sale' Soapy glanced towards his parents.

His mother held an intense stare while Dad was furiously filming everything. So far so good.

When the song ended, onto the stage came two boys from Soapy's class, dressed as undertakers. They struggled to drag a large cardboard coffin with them.

"There we are," said Mr Bumble prodding Soapy. "That's where you are going. I'm selling you to the undertaker as an apprentice. It's dead bodies and funerals for you from now on, ha ha."

Soapy was hauled by the collar and handed over to a grim looking boy who was wearing a stupendously tall hat and a long black coat.

"My name is Mr Sowerberry," said the boy with a quiver in his voice. "This is my assistant, Noah Claypole." He pointed to the second boy whose hat was too big and kept slipping over his eyes. The undertaker then walked off stage with Mr Bumble while Noah Claypole came forward to talk to Soapy.

"I've 'eard that you've got no muvva, kid."

"You leave my mother out of this," said

Soapy. "She's dead."

"I know she's dead, workhouse boy, we buried 'er.'"

"Stop talking about her."

"Best place for 'er, the ground.'"

"Right, you're going to pay for that!" snarled Soapy, thinking that this must be the worst script in the history of theatre. He grabbed Noah Claypole and pushed him down before pretending to pummel him with his fists.

"Helllllp!" screamed Noah and onto the stage rushed Mr Sowerberry who grabbed Soapy and pulled him off his bedraggled assistant.

"How dare you beat my associate," said the undertaker with all the acting skill of a mouldy rug. "Explain yourself, Oliver Twist."

Soapy flicked his eyes about in dread then tried to run but the two boys grabbed him.

"Let's put him in the coffin," said Noah Claypole.

"Good idea," said Mr Sowerberry. "He won't get away from there."

Once more, Soapy showed horror on his face. But this time he wasn't acting. In fact, all three boys turned deathly pale as the lid of the coffin was opened by the undertakers. The audience could not see but there was something inside the casket.

Maggots.

Thousands of white, fat, wriggling maggots.

Soapy gulped. The boys either side of him just stared. The coffin was supposed to be empty. Soapy was supposed to be bundled into it. I am not going to lie down in there. How did this happen? What is going on? Then, Soapy's heart shuddered.

Prankenstein!

For a moment, everything just stopped. Soapy could sense Mr Eckersleight watching from the wings and wondering what the boys were doing, and he heard Chinny clearing his throat, about to prompt them. The audience was silent. He had to do something, he had to rescue the play.

With a sudden movement, Soapy slammed shut the lid of the coffin while the two boys ogled him with bewilderment.

"It's alright, Mr Sowerberry," he said. "I won't run away. No need to put me in the coffin. Er, Noah was right. My mother deserved to die, she was, erm, no good."

There was a murmur from the spectators and Soapy heard Chinny furiously flicking through the script to find the lines he had just made up. The two other actors continued to look wide-eyed with panic.

Soapy continued."Look, I'll just sit here on the coffin, while you go and fetch Mr Bumble, and I'll promise not to escape. Is that alright?"

The boy with the tall hat looked sideways for guidance and saw Mr E nodding rapidly. "Erm, yes, er, alright... er, come on Noah." They shuffled off stage looking confused.

Soapy waited until they were gone then stood up, grinned, and rubbed his hands together, sneaking away from the coffin. The audience giggled approvingly. A wave of relief swept over Soapy as the coffin was dragged off to be replaced by a Victorian street set and on walked Loogi dressed as The Artful

Dodger, top pickpocket of London Town. He wore a tattered blue jacket and an enormous crooked tall hat.

Loogi confidently launched into the next scene, which convinced Soapy that he hadn't seen the maggots, but as his Estonian friend began to sing 'Consider Yourself', all Soapy could consider were the other possible ways that Prankenstein might have booby-trapped the show.

It didn't take long to find out.

In the next scene of the musical, Oliver was taken back to Fagin's den by The Artful Dodger to learn how to become a pickpocket. So Soapy followed

Loogi across the stage to the gloomy set where several boys, including a soot-faced Arvo, were sitting around Mr E who was dressed in a long grubby frock coat and wearing a peculiar pointed beard which was clearly not real.

"Who's this?" said Mr E as Fagin, trying to capture a crooked accent but instead sounding like Bruce Forsyth.

Loogi presented Soapy to the criminal urchins. "This, Fagin and my fellow pickpockets, is Oliver Twist. He is going to be joining us."

"Welcome, Mr Twist," said the hunched Headmaster. "Do you know our business here?"

Soapy looked up at the silk handkerchiefs hanging up around. "Erm is it a laundry?" he said, causing both the pickpockets and the audience to laugh.

"No my boy, we are involved in something rather more, er, lucrative," said Fagin. "Let's explain to him boys."

Soapy knew that this was the cue for the next song, "You've Got to Pick a Pocket or Two", which Mr E usually performed with so much gusto it was embarrassing. As Fagin started to sing he pretended to be a rich city gent walking the street and so he moved towards his hat, hanging on a hook in one corner. Soapy's eyes, flicking everywhere for signs of horrible pranks which would ruin the show and possibly consign him to boarding school, noticed something very odd about Fagin's hat. For a start it looked kind of wet on the inside and shiny or, rather, sticky...

Glue.

He'd seen that before. And there was something else. It was attached to a thin cord of some kind – something like fishing line. That definitely wasn't part of the play, either. He edged closer before Mr E reached the hat. The other end of the string was tied to the coat hook...

Soapy didn't have time to think. As Mr E, in full crafty Fagin mode, came singing and prancing over towards the wide-brimmed hat, his long coat pockets trailing silk hankies and gold watch chains, Soapy grabbed one of the stools from the set and jumped up on it, right in front of the Headteacher, blocking his route.

"You gotta pick a pocket or two-oo," sang Fagin, giving Oliver a questioning look and reaching for the hat. Soapy managed to divert him by leaning forward and slyly grabbing one of the hankies from his coat and draping it over Mr E's face. Once again, the audience laughed at something they didn't expect to see. Soapy then grabbed Fagin's hand and led him away from the hat.

"I gotta pick a pocket or two-oo", sang Soapy, really confusing Mr E, since Oliver wasn't supposed to join in the song at all. The other pickpocket boys, including Loogi and Arvo, looked alarmed but carried on acting by raiding Fagin's pockets to show Oliver how their thievery was done, until at last the song ended and Soapy gave a long sigh of relief. Fagin usually took off the hat at the end of the song anyway so perhaps Prankenstein had been foiled this time.

Soapy could not cope.

# 18
# Hair raising finale

The show carried on, with Soapy watching
out for tricks, pranks, booby-traps and
shenanigans at every turn. In the next act,
Oliver went out into the
streets on a pickpocketing
mission with The Artful
Dodger and ended up being
arrested. Soapy played the
scene with great energy,
aware that he needed to keep
the spotlight on himself and
away from any more fiendish
plots that Prankenstein
might have wormed into
the set and props. Each song
was greeted with rapturous

clapping and the audience were clearly loving the show, despite Oliver's eccentric behaviour in some places.

The story continued on stage and the play's main baddie, Bill Sikes, appeared and eventually kidnapped Oliver after the boy was taken in by a kindly rich man. Soapy was tense, convinced that Prankenstein would ruin it all but nothing unusual happened. Perhaps the maggots and glued hat were all he had planned? It was very odd. After all, it was really he, Soapy, who had done these things and yet he had no recollection of them, no knowledge of whether there might be one last catastrophic prank, primed and in wait to ruin his big evening.

Then something occurred to him.

Venus.

She had already been on stage and tried to steal the show as the baddie's girlfriend, Nancy, who tries to protect Oliver. She sang and danced loudly and flamboyantly, determined to make the watching parents think that she was the great star, the one with all the talent. Perhaps Prankenstein was waiting for her. She still had her last song to sing. Maybe he was going to get her then?

The end of the show drew near and Venus came back onto the stage to sing her final song. Soapy was in a real dilemma. He didn't know whether to want her to be publically pranked or not. She had been so mean to him that she deserved it and yet, it still might ruin everything and cause his parents to send him away.

Venus began to sing, so loud that the scenery shook. Maybe that was it, a giant piece of the stage was cut loose, ready to fall on her giant head? But it didn't happen. Nor did any other pranks. She sang on, throwing her head back and her arms out wide, determined to impress right to the last long note of the song. She had got away with it!

The audience applauded her eagerly, though not quite as eagerly as she would have liked, and then the play moved into its final and darkest part as the evil Bill Sikes kills Nancy on London Bridge as she helps Oliver escape back to the rich gent who had protected him before. Even Soapy had to grimace as the boy playing Bill pretended to whack Venus with a hefty club. He looked at the front row of seats as three boys dressed as Victorian policemen came to rescue him from the clutches of Sikes and signal the last act of the drama as Oliver returned to safety. His mother was smiling. Everybody else was watching intently. And then, swiftly, the final song was finished and the show was over.

There was just a moment's pause before the audience erupted into cheers and applause. Soapy's Mum and Dad stood up followed by everybody else, still cheering and clapping loudly.

It was a triumph. The full cast then came back
onto the stage to bow, with Soapy in the centre,
and still the parents applauded and smiled.
Then a sense of relief almost overwhelmed him
and just for a moment he thought he was going
to collapse.

Prankenstein had been beaten! He hadn't
ruined the show!

Mr E, himself beaming with pride, then
ushered each group of actors to step forward
in turn so they could bow to the audience
and receive their own ovation. The minor

characters went first – the workhouse boys, the pickpockets, Mr Sowerberry and Noah Claypole the undertakers, Mr Bumble, and so on, before the main players stepped forward. Soapy wasn't sure when to go but the headmaster held him back. Perhaps he, as the leading role was going to be last, for the biggest cheer of all? He wasn't sure whether he wanted that or not. Venus certainly did, and Soapy noticed her annoyance when Mr E sent her forward before she put on a false smile and cavorted to the front, waving wildly and for far too long to the spectators.

After Bill Sikes had been, that left just Mr E himself and Soapy to receive their moment of glory. Mr E suddenly pushed Soapy forward, obviously keeping the final call for himself. But Soapy didn't care, the audience erupted into a huge cheer as he stepped to the front of the stage and clapped until their hands were sore. He was amazed and wonderfully happy. Even his mother looked proud. Surely boarding school was now dead.

Then he stepped back and the line of child actors parted for Fagin to come through. Mr E was determined to enjoy his big moment and why not? The production had been an enormous success. Soapy certainly didn't mind – after all, the show had saved his bacon. Mr E once more went into full Fagin mode, dancing and prancing as the parents hoorayed. Soapy tried to catch the eye of Arvo and Loogi so he could give them the thumbs up, and in doing so he failed to spot the Headmaster suddenly realising that part of his costume was missing

and scooting to the side of the stage to pick up his hat from the hook where it still hung.

As Mr E rammed the hat down onto his head and dallied forward with one last crooked Fagin shuffle to thank the audience, Soapy turned around. He was just in time to see the string, tied to both the hat and the coat hook, begin to rise and then pull tight as the school's happy Head capered to the front.

There was no time to do anything. As Mr E reached the edge of the stage with arms out wide, his tragic hairpiece took off like a bushy missile attached to a wide brimmed hat, leaving a gloss-domed head and a speechless audience.

Well, they were only speechless for a moment. A hullabaloo of snorting mirth filled the air as everyone laughed at the poor bald principal who couldn't quite comprehend what had happened.

Everyone except one, that is. Soapy closed his eyes and envisaged a life of Latin, canes and the insides of toilets. I'm doomed.

Prankenstein had triumphed after all.

# 19
# Venus tells tales

Soapy hid in the toilets after the show, not daring to speak to Arvo and Loogi with all the teachers around and Venus lurking. The thought of what his parents would say was so frightening that he shut it out of his mind completely. He let his imagination take over and found a perfect distraction by making up newspaper headlines about the events of the night:

HEAD'S HEAD DEAD RED
WIG WHAM!
FAGIN FLAMIN' FURIOUS
WHAT THE DICKENS!
SHOW SHAMBLES SHOCKER
OLIVER LAUGH

## TOUPEE PRANK LEAVES SCHOOL BOSS WITH BARE NOGGIN AFTER MUSICAL TRIUMPH.

Soapy decided that the last one would probably be in the Financial Times.

Eventually, he left the toilet cubicle knowing that his parents would be waiting for him. There was no putting it off any longer. He wondered what Chinny and Mr E were going to do about the theatrical prank as he wandered through the now empty cloakroom. As Soapy opened the hall door he gulped. There were his mum and dad, replaying the video of the show on their camcorder. Everyone else had gone. He wandered towards them slowly, trying not to look frightened.

"Pugh, there you are!"

"Erm, hi Mum."

Dad's face lit up "You were sensational!"

"Oh, er, was I?"

"Son, you were a star – I knew you had it in you."

"But, er-"

"Lots of people congratulated us." interrupted

his mum, "I have to say I had no idea you could perform so, well, entertainingly."

Soapy plucked up the courage to ask the question that was hammering away inside his brain.

"What about Mr Eckersleight's, erm, accident at the end of the show?"

Dad looked over his shoulder and chuckled. "The wig prank, you mean? That was hair-larious!"

Mum put her finger to her lips. "Jake, keep your voice down, he might be around." She added in a whisper. "Even I laughed at that – and I told you he wore a hairpiece."

"Poor fella," said Dad, smiling and shaking his head slowly.

Soapy didn't know what to say. "So, you enjoyed the show then. All of it?"

Dad ruffled his hair.

"We told you. It was fantastic."

"So, you're not going to send me to boarding school, then?"

Mum gave a nod. "Well, we'd better stick to our side of the deal – boarding school is off."

Soapy breathed deeply and gave a silent prayer of thanks.

"Come on, let's get home," said Mum, "I want to watch you again on the screen."

As they turned towards the exit, the hall door opened and Venus Bray appeared almost dragging the school's Headteacher who had somehow managed to acquire another wig. Soapy's first thought was that she was still furious about being upstaged at the end of the show.

"I told you they were still here, Mr E," she said, her eyes full of fire.

"Is there a problem?" said Mum, her brow knitted.

Mr E held up an apologetic hand. "I'm sorry, Mr and Mrs Thompson, but Venus here insists that I talk to you, even though it's late."

"What's it about?" said Dad. Soapy felt his chest tighten.

"Well... er-"

Venus jumped in. "I know who did the pranks. It was him." She pointed at Soapy. 'He's been doing them for weeks.'

"She's insistent, I'm afraid," said Mr E. "And there have been a lot of, well, strange things going on."

Soapy felt his legs wobble and a sensation like there was no blood in his head. He wondered if he was about to faint but a hand went to his shoulder and he saw his mother raise herself up and go into full serious lawyer mode.

"This is quite an accusation, Venus. We'd better ask him first. Pugh, are you responsible for all these pranks that have been going on recently?"

He hesitated for a moment and then the words came. "It wasn't me."

"Liar," said Venus.

"Please!" called Mum sharply. She looked Soapy in the eye. "Did you do any of the pranks?"

"None of them were me, they were someone else."

Mum turned to the headmaster. "Well, we have been over this before at home, Mr Eckersleight, and he's denied it consistently." She looked at Venus. "Do you have any proof?"

"I've heard him talking about pranks."

Soapy held out his hands. "Everyone's been talking about pranks!"

"That's true, ahem," said Mr E.

Dad threw up his arms. "Oh come on, this is spoiling Soapy's big night. If Venus hasn't actually seen him doing any of the pranks then how can she be so sure?"

Venus's mouth was puckered and her cheeks fury-red."I just know it's him."

Soapy sensed his chance. "How could I have added a V8 engine to Granny's stairlift? I can't even get my Lego box open. And how could I have changed Mr Chinn's teeth or climbed the town hall? I'm just not that brave."

Mum gave a little nod. "He does have a strong point. What do you think, Headmaster?"

Mr E exhaled. He looked worn out. "I just don't see how it's possible." He regarded Venus. "I wonder if the burden of doing this TV show along with the theatre auditions and the musical tonight has just been too much for this young lady. It's your big final tomorrow, so you'd better get home and get a good night's sleep, Venus."

Soapy's parents nodded in agreement and Venus turned and stomped out of the hall muttering that she was right and would prove it. Everyone could see Mr and Mrs Bray hovering the other side of the doors looking sheepish. Soapy slumped with relief. Nobody believes Venus!

The car journey home didn't go so well. The excitement of the show's success had been completely squashed by Venus's claim. His parents had backed him up and yet there hung in the air a lingering suspicion and he knew that his mum in particular would be thinking hard about why Venus would have accused Soapy. It didn't take long to come up.

"Have you done something to Venus, Pugh?" said his mother.

"What do you mean?"

"I mean something to upset her. Have you said something nasty or hurt her in some way?"

"No, it's the other way round, honest, Mum. I admit I don't like her but she's the bully – she's always calling me names, laughing at my phone and boasting."

"Then doesn't that give you a reason for playing pranks on her?"

"No, well, yes, but I haven't."

Dad looked back. "You have to admit, dear, she is loud and a total show off. Maybe she's jealous because Soapy outshone her in Oliver!"

Good old Dad thought Soapy, continuing his own defence. "She thinks I'm not cool either because I'm not interested in all the celebrity stuff she's obsessed with."

Mum looked thoughtful. "Well, I can see that. But, all the same, for her to accuse you in front of the Headteacher of doing all these pranks is very odd. I agree that you can't have done them all but I'm still suspicious, young man, and we shall be watching you like a hawk for a while. Got that?"

I hate it when she says 'young man'.

"Yes, Mum."

During the rest of the journey his mind was numb with emotion, then as they turned into the drive an unpleasant, thumping, growling fear hit him.

What if Prankenstein strikes again tonight?

# 20
# Searching for cheese

As soon as he got into his room Soapy called the Twince. Arvo was already asleep but Loogi answered.

"Man, you were sensational!"

"Thanks," said Soapy.

"Everyone was going rave about your performance."

"Well, not everyone. Venus Bray accused me of doing the pranks, right in front of my parents and Mr E."

"Whaaat! What did you say?"

"I said it wasn't me."

"Well, that's kind of truthful."

"My dad and Mr E believed me but my mum is still suspicious. She said she's going to watch me like a hawk."

"You mean she's going to flap around from a great height then peck you?"

"Loogi, this is no time for jokes. Didn't you see what happened with Mr E's wig?"

"Of course; my pants nearly came off laughing. Oh, I see. It was…"

"…Prankenstein. He's started again."

"Ah, does that explain why you also changed the Oliver story with the coffin on stage?"

"Exactly."

Soapy went on to explain about the maggots and the glue and string and how he'd woken up with a headache that morning.

"But you are saying it was a different headache from the ones before?" asked Loogi.

"Yes, but it signalled the same thing."

"Okay, I am thinking more detective work

is required here...well, we cannot blame the Mini-Bels because you ensured the destruction of them."

"I know, I threw them in the lake. It's a mystery."

"Prankenstein must have obtained other cheese – ah, that is probably why the headache felt different.

"That makes sense, but how?"

"Are you sure there is no cheese in the house?"

"Completely sure, my mum and dad never take any chances."

"Then Prankenstein must have found some and done stashing somewhere nearby."

"It could be... but what if I sleepwalk tonight? There'll be more pranks – probably some massive ones here at home and my parents will be on the lookout. If they discover what's happening then it's boarding school for sure. That means I'll never see you two – I'll be locked in some crumbling old mansion with a load of toffs."

"Hey, Mr Soapy Thompson, correct my

wrongness if need be, but was it not you declaring in recent times that you were missing Prankenstein and his jelly japes?"

"I was talking rubbish. Total trash. Garbage. And it's jolly japes. I can't take the strain, Loogi. I have this horrible feeling that Prankenstein is going to get my mum tonight too."

"Why is that?"

"Well because she's so suspicious and annoying. I'm worried that somehow Prankenstein knows this – like you said, he's my dark side and he does all the bad things I'd secretly like to do but am too afraid."

"That would be not good."

"Very not good." "Okay, don't worry, I am plan hatching. I will wake Arvo later and we'll sneak out and come round to yours when everyone is asleep – we will search the house."

"Really? That would be so good, Loogi. But it's a big risk for you two."

"Hey, you were not the only star of the musical show tonight, boy. There were a certain two pickpockets that made the wow of certain Estonian parents. Even if we are captured, I think we can escape the brute punishment." His tone then became more serious. "Anyway, we don't want to lose a good friend."

Soapy swallowed. "Okay, what time shall we meet?"

"See you at two o'clock – rendezvous behind the garage."

"Who is Ron de Voo? Another friend from Estonia?"

"No, it means meeting: you should know your own language."

"Oh, rendezvous. That's French."

"Whatever. 2am, bye."

Soapy put down his mobile and gave a sigh.

You can't beat proper friends.

A knock at the door startled him. Dad popped his head into the room.

"We're just about to put the video of the show on, are you coming down to watch it?"

"Isn't it, er, a bit late?" Soapy looked at his watch which said 9.40pm.

"Well, yes, but it is Friday and it's been such an exciting evening that we'll let you stay up specially."

The last thing he wanted was to sit through the show again, reliving the torment of covering up Prankenstein's schemes. "Actually, I think I'll go to bed – all the excitement of the play has made me extra tired." He feigned a yawn and rubbed his eyes.

"Well, okay, but it's a shame. Ivette and her boyfriend are watching it with us too."

"What about Granny?"

"She can see it tomorrow. Your mum's going to pick her up then, and we're all watching Venus in the final of Stars of Tomorrow here in the evening. Don't forget that includes you

— I know it's difficult after what happened earlier but we promised the Brays that we'd all vote."

Soapy felt queasy as he said good night and Dad closed the door.

I wish that girl would go and find another planet.

It was surprisingly cold outside for a summer's night and Soapy shivered as he waited for the Twince to appear in the gloom behind the garage. It had been hard to stay awake for the four hours in his room after Dad left. Soapy could hear the adults downstairs laughing at the video and opening bottles of wine. At one stage he began to fear that they might actually stay up until 2am and discover the plan but soon after midnight they switched everything off and noisily climbed the stairs after Ivette's boyfriend left the house.

As Soapy waited he tried out his small head torch to see if still worked. It did but he wondered whether his friends would bring some sort of lamp too. Searching without one would be useless. To pass the time he imagined a conversation:

*Soapy: Hi boys – are you ready?*
*Loogi: Yes, I have a torch.*
*Soapy: That's good, what about you, Arvo?*
*Arvo: I am bringing a carrot*
*Soapy: Why have you brought a carrot?*
*Arvo: My auntie says they help you to see*
*in the dark.*

The brothers arrived a little late, wearing dark clothes and carrying small but bright LED lights and no root vegetables. Arvo was yawning.

"We are sorry for the time," said Loogi in a whisper. "First Arvo's battery was flattened then I needed the toilet."

"And you nearly did the foolish flushing. That would have woken our parents and raised up large suspicions," said Arvo just a little too loudly.

Soapy put his finger to his lips. "Shhh, it doesn't matter, you're both here now and we'd better get looking for cheese."

"Who is in the house?" said Arvo.

"My mum and dad are in and so is Ivette,

so it's going to be really difficult to search inside."

"We two cannot risk going in there in case we do bumpings and bangings against objects which are not familiar," said Loogi, looking serious.

"Correct," said Arvo. "We had better make a garden search and you Soapy examine the house. Have we agreement?"

They all nodded and arranged to meet back by the garage at 3am.

"I'll do the upstairs first," said Soapy, yawning as he realised that he was exhausted after the strain of the musical and everything that followed it.

The Twince checked that the curtains were closed so that they couldn't be seen from the house while Soapy sneaked back inside, opening and closing the door in slow motion.

"I'll begin looking in the shed, you search under that hedge," said Loogi, for once taking the lead as the brothers slunk across the patio.

Arvo switched on his torch. "Acceptable plan. Hey, I am starting to enjoy this now I'm

more awake. Do you think we are in danger
of being caught?"

"Well, we do have the appearance of burglars
but if arrested we could perhaps inform the police
force that this is a game we are playing with
Soapy," whispered Loogi, opening the shed door
with great care. "That is kind of true, anyways."

"The game is 'Find the Cheese'," said Arvo.
"Yeah, most probably the English invented this
anyway, along with football, tennis, railways,
Monty Python and the beery oik."

Loogi wasn't listening. He'd already spotted
something unusual at the back of the shed – a
small shiny object. It was a piece of aluminium
foil. He picked it up and noticed immediately
that it was heavy. He put down his torch and
carefully opened the small package.

"Whoah!"

The smell knocked him backwards into
a pile of seed trays. Arvo heard the noise and
came rushing over.

NOTE: 'Beery oik' is a name used for a man who likes guzzling beer and watching football.

"Quiet! You are being nutter and they will hear us. What's that?"

"Surely you can whiff it?"

"Otch! I can now – I recall this is Hilton is it not?

"Not. That is hotel of swank. I think it is Spilton or perhaps Shilton," murmured Loogi.

"Ah, no, Shilton is that bad perm Eighties goalkeeper. He is in my World Cup book."

Loogi put up a finger. "Stilton! Remember, Mum produced a sandwich with this one time. It nearly blew out our eyeballs."

"Quite possible," nodded Arvo. "Well, it is cheese, that is for sure, and I am concluding that this is a stash of Prankenstein."

"And we have discovered only a small amount here. There is probably more elsewhere. Perhaps this is the moment to text Soapy?"

"No, someone might hear his phone. Let's first see if we can find some more."

In the next 40 minutes, the boys unearthed sixteen small foil packages of ponky blue-veined cheese. It was beneath hedges, under leaves, behind bushes, even in holes in trees. They looked for a further ten minutes but found no more. Arvo checked his watch.

"It is just beyond 3pm. We must return to the garage."

There was no sign of their friend when they arrived so the boys waited, rubbing their arms from time to time to keep warm.

"I wonder what has happened to Soapy?" muttered Arvo.

"Come, we should make way to his window," said Loogi, flicking on his torch again.

The window was slightly open and they could see a dim light behind the curtain but there was no sign of movement. It was too risky to call up to him. They wondered if he'd been discovered, but decided that he would have texted them if that had happened. They waited a little while longer then risked sending a text themselves.

There was no answer.

The brothers waited another five minutes then edged around to the back door and, with trembling fingers, pulled the handle downwards. It was open. Both boys could feel their insides tensing as they inched through the kitchen, past the living room and ascended the stairs with maximum stealth.

With gulps of silent breath they reached Soapy's door and gently pushed it open. What they saw made them stop dead.

On Soapy's desk, lit by his lamp, were six small foil packages. One of them was open, and empty. The window was off its latch. The bed was ruffled.

Soapy was gone.

# 21
# Star of tomorrow?

Arvo and Loogi gathered up the cheese and crept out of the house swiftly, heading back towards their own home. Wearing frowns, they wondered about their friend as they walked.

"This is not good. Soapy was probably finding the cheese but then somehow fell asleep also," said Arvo. "He did have a look of exhaustion after the play."

"I think he finished searching the house and then perhaps sat down for a rest."

"Yes, this is a possibility. He likely dropped asleep while waiting for 3 o'clock."

Loogi nodded. "Then came the sleepwalking again..."

"...And the consuming of the Spilton."

"Stilton."

"Yes." The boys slowed down and looked at each other before Loogi spoke.

"This means that Prankenstein is out and about tonight... He could be watching us right now." Each boy felt a shiver down his spine. They looked around and increased their pace.

A minute later they passed a skip outside a house. It was full of rubble.

"Ah, look, let's secrete the cheese in here," said Arvo. "We can bury it under these bricks."

Loogi wondered whether they were being observed as they rearranged the heavy debris in the skip. A cat skulked out of the gloom and made him jump. He looked at Arvo.

"Perhaps like I, you have realised something?"

"What?"

"That almost certainly Prankenstein has already been on the prank tonight. And, even if we have removed all of the cheese from Soapy's home, that humanoid beastie could be stealing some more right of it now."

"I know. This could be going on and on."

"Poor Soapy – with Venus looking for proof

and his mother watching him like the eagle, he is sure to be found out eventually."

"Correct, and if Prankenstein is discovered then terrible things will happen to our friend."

"If he is being sent to boarding school or prison we may never see him again."

"Well at least it is Saturday tomorrow," said Arvo, yawning once more. "I suppose we can sneak round in the morning and check the shed and garden again."

Loogi bit his lip. "Okay, but we cannot go on with this cheese detection each day. Something has to be done."

The boys didn't know it, of course, but something was being done at that precise moment, less than a mile away across town.

Venus Bray was sitting up in bed with a look of despair while her mother fretted around her in a dressing gown, trying to stay calm.

"Venus, it's half past three, this is the middle of the night for goodness' sake. You must try to get back to sleep. We've got to drive to London mid-morning."

"It's no good, I've tried, I just can't get to sleep, Mum – I'm too excited about the show tomorrow. I can't believe I'm going to be live on TV. It will be amazing... millions of people watching... the cheering audience... singing in a proper big studio... and I'm going to meet Dijon Sparkes again!"

"You are a star, precious, but even stars need sleep, especially when it's the final of the show tomorrow."

"I'm going to win Mum. Nothing can stop me. I just know it. I'm the best there, easily – I'll be rich and famous."

"Well, I just hope you're not disappointed, darling. Anyway, it's good that you're wearing the sequin dress and not the gold suit. It's even classier."

Venus wasn't listening. "I've just had a thought. When I win, the West End theatre people are bound to give me a good part in The Jungle Book – then I won't have to do any more of those stupid auditions."

"Don't get ahead of yourself, Vee; I really

don't think things are that simple in life and
you haven't won yet."

Venus sat up with a sneer across her mouth.
"What do you know, mother? You've never been
in show business. I think I know more than you!"

"Venus there is no need to be rude. Look,
I'm going to make you a hot chocolate. Perhaps
that will help get you to sleep."

Mrs Bray went downstairs while Venus visited
to the loo then brushed her hair in the bathroom.
Her mother returned with a steaming mug of
cocoa and, seeing her daughter's bed empty,
left it on her bedside cabinet before returning
to her own bed.

The sounds of doors opening and closing,
footsteps on the landing and running taps
travelled out through the slightly open window
of Venus's room and into the cool night air
where they were detected by a large, grizzled
ear pressed close to the wall below. Just beneath
the ear was a fat, warty hand. The hand was
clenched tight around something.

With remarkable agility a dark, hairy

figure leapt upwards onto the wooden sill and pulled open the window, disappearing inside. Just a few seconds later it reappeared, closed the window and bounded down, dropping something into the garden before melting away into the night. Three small, empty packets nestled behind a laurel bush and each one bore the same blue writing:

MR TROUSER TRUMPET'S EXTRA STRENGTH FART POWDER

Momentous bottom barking guaranteed

Venus returned to her room, slipped under the covers and once more pictured herself being announced as the winner of Stars of Tomorrow, live on national television. As she closed her eyes, the warm, creamy smell of hot chocolate reached her nostrils. She turned and took a sip from the cup. It was delicious.

Late the following morning Soapy was

awoken by the sound of a text on his mobile. It was the Twince saying that they were coming over at 11.00 if that was OK with him. It was probably OK, but at that moment he didn't really care about anything apart from getting rid of the dull ache that

was grinding inside his head.

He opened the curtains and it gradually came back to him. The school musical, the wig, Venus, the cheese and now... what? He didn't want to know. He just wanted to bop Prankenstein over the head with something large.

The brothers arrived soon after a breakfast of hot lemon. Fortunately, Dad was out playing golf, Mum was shopping and it was Ivette's day off.

"Has there been any pranking?" said Arvo, looking about. "Soapy, you have the look of the terrible."

"I feel the terrible. I don't think Prankenstein did anything here or my parents would have woken me up for questioning."

"Can you remember anything from last night," said Loogi.

"Not really, just finding the Stilton packages and then, er, falling asleep."

"Anyhow, we had better start the hunt for cheese again while there is a clear coast," said Arvo.

The three boys once more searched his bedroom and then the shed and garden.

"I can't keep doing this," said Soapy, pushing over a bag of compost. "It's not funny anymore."

'Well, actually, we were about to say the same thing,' said Arvo. "We have not found any cheese this time but this fool monster could have hidden it anywhere."

Loogi nodded. "We cannot keep coming here to find and destroy cheeses or our parents will know we are something up to, especially if the pranks continue."

"And I cannot face the sneaking out late at night," added Arvo. "That was fun once but it is way too much risky and tiring. We're are sorry, Soapy, but you must do the dealing with Prankenstein yourself somehow."

The three of them stood in silence for a minute, contemplating trouble and misery. It wasn't long coming.

"Pu-ugh!"

"It's my mum," said Soapy. "She's probably heard on the local news about some crazy incident and wants to find out if I know anything." The friends ambled out towards the back door where she was standing.

"I hope you haven't been in the shed boys. There are tools in there with edges, you know. And what have you been doing, Pugh? You look ghastly. Anyway, don't tell me now because I'm in a hurry. I'll have to take Arvo and Loogi home in a minute because we've got to go and pick up Grandma. Your father's at golf and

Ivette's out so I can't leave you on your own."

"But I was on my own when I woke up."

"You mean your father just went out and left you?"

"Mum, I'm eleven, and I've watched all the Bear Grylls DVDs. I can survive an hour in a warm house."

"What if the boiler blew up or some fraudsters came to the door or you tried to use the wrong kind of knife to make toast? And, what's more, you could have been up to anything."

'Mum, I am alright; nothing happened and we haven't been up to anything: it's been very, er, peaceful here.' He glanced sideways at the Twince while Mum's needle-like eyes pierced him, making it clear that she was still on hawk duty.

'Hmmm, I do hope so. Anyway, let's all get in the car, it's late.' She stepped inside before turning back to the boys. 'And double check the seatbelts.'

As they drove towards the Twince' house Soapy's mum kept up a stream of tiresome reminders.

'Don't plan anything for this evening, Pugh, because remember we're showing grandma your Oliver! highlights and watching the Stars of Tomorrow final together.'

Soapy made a puking face across the back seat towards the Twince.

'This car is equipped with a mirror, Pugh Thompson.'

Arvo stifled a snigger but Soapy was too depressed to laugh, especially as his mother continued her lecture.

"I know that you don't get on with Venus but she is our friends' daughter and we should all be supporting her in this competition, and that includes you. So don't be mean and nasty."

Soapy pondered. If only you knew how mean and nasty I am sometimes.

At seven o'clock Soapy found himself wedged between Granny and Dad on the settee in front of the TV. She'd been there for an hour and had already said three times that he looked like Winston Churchill as a baby. Dad was in a bad mood because he was arguing with

Mum about whether they should vote for Venus over the phone.

He shook his head. "It's a pound a go and it won't make any difference anyway. There are millions of votes."

"Well, I think we should. We said we would and it was you who were sticking up for the Brays before – all that golf buddy stuff." Mum's mouth twitched.

"I'm voting for Soapy," said Granny.

Dad folded his arms. "I've changed my mind about Venus Bray since she made that ridiculous accusation about the pranks." He looked at his wife. "You hate this show, anyway."

Mum tried to hide her irritation, probably for Granny's sake. "Shush now, it's starting."

The TV screen flashed with spotlights and sparkle and the maddening Stars of Tomorrow theme music came on along with the blinding white teeth of blonde host Dijon Sparkes followed by images of various desperate child performers.

Soapy sighed. No please carry on, Dad.

Even family arguments are better than this.

The show was worse than he had feared. The first act was a boy who juggled balls of earwax whilst eating a prune muffin. This was followed by a group of Welsh girl guides who played 'God Save The Queen' using spatulas. And they were the best ones.

Perhaps Prankenstein had an accident last night and I've died and gone to hell.

Mum kept going out to make a surprisingly large number of cups of coffee but at least Granny seemed to be enjoying it, although she did keep asking why the contestants were so small. Soapy tried to get away with pretending he had fallen asleep but a swift elbow in the ribs from Dad thwarted that plan.

"Here's Venus – turn it up a bit."

Soapy barely recognised her under an extraordinary layer of makeup. "It looks like a voodoo mask."

"Give her a chance," said Mum, who was finding it hard to disguise her own revulsion at the sight.

Dijon Sparkes, who looked about eight foot tall next to all the child finalists boomed out, "And now, contestant six, it's eleven year old Venus Bray singing ABBA's 'Super Trouper'!" There was a cacophony of whoops and hollers above the applause as the introduction to the music began. Venus's smile was barely contained by the wide-screen TV as she launched into her song with enough energy to power a bacon factory.

Even Soapy, much as he hated the idea, had to admit that she had a good voice. She's not shy either, he thought, as she threw back her head and held out her arms.

It was when she launched into the chorus a second time that something strange happened. Venus was meant to sing the word 'beams' but for some reason she said 'beans'. Her movements were becoming odd too. She started leaning sideways and she kept squeezing her eyes closed.

"Her singing's gone a bit funny," said Dad.

Soapy was suddenly interested. "Yes, she's really straining to get the words out."

"She looks like she's going to explode," said Granny.

It soon became clear that it wasn't words that she was straining to get out. Venus reached the end of a verse and then lifted a leg, her teeth clenched.

"Ooh, she's going to do the Hokey Cokey," said Granny. "I like that."

The music was loud but above it there came a thundering rumble followed by an ear-splitting blast unmistakable to the seven million viewers watching.

Soapy was really enjoying the show now. "What's this song? 'Super Trumper'?"

Mum looked aghast. "I think she's having a spasm."

"I just hope it doesn't become 'Super Pooper'," said Dad, who was wiping away the tears of laughter streaming down his face.

"Do you think it'll get to number one," said Granny.

"I think a number two is more likely," snorted Soapy.

Venus was now doing more wafting than singing and the studio audience was in uproar as she helplessly let out another volley of booming guffs.

"She's by far the most entertaining," said Dad.

The camera showed the face of the head judge who looked like he had just discovered

something unpleasant on the sole of his shoe.
Then it closed in on Dijon Sparkes, who was
doubled over with laughter and unable to
speak. Finally Venus once more filled the
screen, gamely singing the last word of the

song before letting out one final high-pitched ripper. The audience stood up and roared with applause. Dad joined in. Soapy cheered. Venus fainted.

"ABBA are not as good as they used to be," said Granny.

# 22
# A deadly pill

"Wakey, wakey, it's half past nine," said Mum, gently prodding Soapy's shoulder.

For a moment he felt a surge of panic about being late for school and then he remembered it was Sunday. "Can't I have a longer lie in?"

"Well, I suppose so – you must be extra tired after what you did last night."

His heart fluttered and he sat up rapidly. "Last night, what d'you mean?"

"Well I heard a bit of a noise on the landing at about 2am and went to have a look. It was you sleepwalking again. You haven't done that for a while."

"Er, well, I suppose it could happen, er, anytime. What did I look like?"

"What do you mean what did you look like? You looked the same as you always do, except wearing pyjamas."

"Oh, so I didn't look, erm, different? Hairy or anything?"

"I don't know what you mean, Pugh. Anyway, I've spoken to your father and we can't have you wandering around the house at night like you used to. Imagine the accidents and the chaos that could happen."

Soapy nodded. "You're right there, Mum."

"So, anyway, I've phoned the surgery and the doctor on call there said that there are pills you can have to stop you doing it. I'm going out to get you some later this morning."

"To stop me sleepwalking?"

"Yes."

"You can get pills for it?"

"That's what I just said. So it's no more sleepwalking adventures for you." Her eyes widened as a colossal grin broke out across her son's face. "You seem very pleased about it, anyway."

As soon as he could, Soapy threw on some clothes and rushed outside away from his parents' hearing. Punching the keys on his mobile he called the Twince.

"Hi Soapy," said Arvo. "What is it now – more pranking? We can't come to hunt for cheese again. We've told you."

"No, it's not that. It's great news."

"What do you mean?"

"Prankenstein is dead!"

"Eh?"

"It's all over. He's gone forever!"

Loogi came on the line. "But how did you do him in?"

"It wasn't me – it was my mum. She's getting me pills to stop sleepwalking, today!"

"Really?"

"Yes! No more sleepwalking, no more cheese, no more pranks! They were fun but there is only so much fun a boy can take."

"We are agreeing with this," said the

Twince together.

"And now Venus Bray will never be able to prove it was me who did all that stuff – I'm safe. We're safe!"

"You're right," said Arvo. "We won't lose you to Eton or Alcatraz now."

"I was worried that he was going to do some awful prank to my mum but nothing's happened. It really is goodbye Prankenstein."

"As long as you are taking the tablets, of course," added Loogi.

For once, Dad hadn't gone to golf and the whole family sat down together for a late Sunday breakfast, even Ivette. They all sensed that Soapy was in a magnificent mood and this made everyone smile. Never had he enjoyed a bowl of wild porridge with Total Bran so much.

"I rang the Brays this morning," said Mum. "I wondered if Venus was alright after, er, not winning the show."

"She came second, though," said Dad, smiling.

"What did they say?" said Soapy.

"Well, I spoke to Graham and he told me

that Venus is giving up auditions and entering these contests. She just wants to be an ordinary girl and do kids' stuff," he said.'

"Won't she miss the singing?" asked Ivette, who Soapy thought secretly wanted to be a pop star.

"Mr Bray said she's fed up with it. She just wants to be normal and not to have that awful pressure. The Super Trouper trauma just finished her off."

Soapy smiled. "The wind of change..."

"Nice one, son," said Dad, although Mum frowned.

As they ate their wholemeal toast and drank their fruit tea they were quite unaware that, 20 miles away, the City Zoo was minus one of its prize animals and that, right at that moment, the keepers and police were trying to solve the mystery.

Indeed, it was hard to say who was in for the biggest shock that morning. Soapy's mum, as she headed for the utility room to find some more fig juice, or the 223kg mountain gorilla on the other side of the door.